AS WE NEARED THE INN, UNCLE PATRICK
BEGAN TO WHISTLE SOME JAUNTY TUNE, A
SAILOR'S HORNPIPE, I THOUGHT.

"And is it happy you are to be at sea again?" I
asked.

He chuckled. "Faith, at least I'm happy to see you
happy." He paused at the inn door and clapped a
hand on my shoulder. "Only understand this, Davy
Shea: You are not to expect every day aboard a king's
ship to be a holiday. No, it's bad food, work, and
blessed hard work at that, with long hours, and a fair
chance of drowning or being blown to kingdom
come, all thrown into the bargain. Not to mention
bloody decks that don't stay in the same place from
one second to the next."

"Sir," I said, "I'm looking forward to it."

And Lord help me, on that eighteenth of August,
so I was, having no notion at all of the terrible great
change that just three short weeks could make.

Mutiny!

Brad Strickland and Thomas E. Fuller

ALADDIN PAPERBACKS
New York London Toronto Sydney Singapore

Affectionately dedicated to my oldest son, Edward Stewart Fuller
—*Thomas E. Fuller*

To my son, Jonathan Strickland
—*Brad Strickland*

First Aladdin Paperbacks edition November 2002

Text copyright © 2002 by Brad Strickland and Thomas E. Fuller
Illustrations copyright © 2002 by Dominic Saponaro

ALADDIN PAPERBACKS
An imprint of Simon & Schuster
Children's Publishing Division
1230 Avenue of the Americas
New York, NY 10020

Designed by Debra Sfetsios
The text of this book was set in Minion.

Printed in the United States of America
2 4 6 8 10 9 7 5 3 1

Library of Congress Control Number 2002102015

ISBN 0-689-85296-7

PIRATE HUNTER

Mutiny!

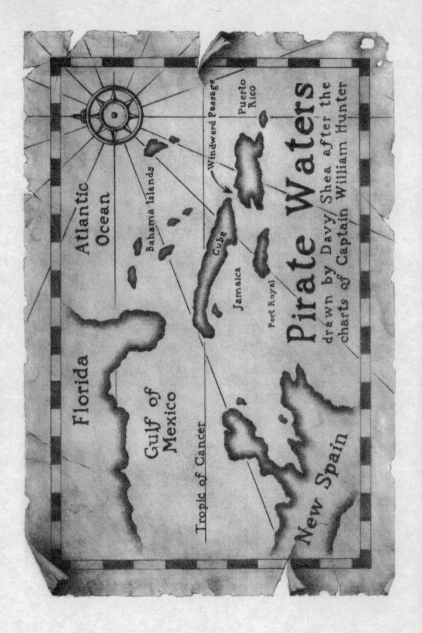

Pirate Waters

drawn by Davy Shea after the charts of Captain William Hunter

Florida

Atlantic Ocean

Gulf of Mexico

Tropic of Cancer

Bahama Islands

Windward Passage

Puerto Rico

Cuba

Jamaica

Port Royal

New Spain

Main Mast

Mizzen

Fore

Rigging

Crows Nest

Captain's Cabin

Stern

Bow

CHAPTER ONE

The King's Mercy

SOMEONE WAS SHAKING me out of a fitful sleep. I opened my eyes and saw very little more than darkness with only a faint flicker of crimson. The man who had one hand on my shoulder was, with the other hand, holding up a lantern with a stubby inadequate candle in it. In the dark, stinking orlop of the merchant ship *Louisa*, the candle burned so ill that it was more a glow, feeble and red, than a light.

"David Shea!" the figure slurred, his gin-soaked breath as much as his voice revealing him to be the Reverend Mr. Bonney. "David Shea! Wake up! We're anchored in Port Royal! Stir your lazy shanks, boy!"

Groaning, I swung out of my hammock. My bare feet hit the splintery wood of the deck, and I heard a skitter in the darkness. "What's that?" I asked.

"Just rats, David, just some of God's humbler creatures!"

Rats. Some of the sailors hunted them, killed them, and ate them. Six weeks at sea had not yet given me a taste for rat.

"Here!" The Reverend Mr. Bonney shoved a bundle into my hands. Even half-asleep, I recognized it. It was my canvas seabag, and it held my few worldly possessions: two shirts, two pair of breeches, smallclothes, stockings, and the suit and pair of shoes the good Mr. Horne had bought for me to wear to my mother's funeral. Those, and the clothes I stood in, were all I owned. Mr. Bonney shook me again.

"Are you awake?"

"Yes, sir," I said.

The minister gave me a rough shove. "Lazy, like all boys. That won't do now, lad. You'll need your wits about you." Mr. Bonney reached into his pocket and then shook a small gray cloth purse in my face. It jangled. "And you'll need this. 'Tis the money Mr. Horne gave me to keep for you." Before I could take it, he'd thrust it deep into my seabag, pulled the drawstring tight, and tied it. "There, that'll keep it safe for you. On deck, now. Look lively, look lively! It's just touch and go here."

He led the way aft, then up a narrow companionway. I followed, hoping for fresher air—for I was heartily sick of the sweaty, smelly atmosphere of the closed-in lower deck the sailors called the orlop. But we were fairly in the Caribbees, on the southern coast of Jamaica, and the night was tropical, heavy, and moist. I looked up at the dark sky. Thin clouds half-hid a waxing moon, making it a smudged white thumbprint on the face of the night. No stars at all. Mr. Bonney hauled at my arm. "Here he is!"

"Sir—Mr. Bonney," I said desperately, "where am I to find my uncle Patrick?"

He snorted in annoyance, and the sharp odor of gin poured over me again. "Doing some wild, papish, heathenish business, no doubt." The minister was on his way to preach the Gospel on some island or other. Mr. Horne had assured me that Mr. Bonney would take care of me during our voyage.

So far as I could tell, his "taking care" of me consisted merely of constantly losing small sums of money playing at dice or cards with the sailors, drinking too much, and looking sour each time he saw me. He pulled me toward a group of men at the rail and growled, "He's said to stay at the inn called The King's Mercy. That is in Thames Street, and that is all I know. You men, there! Here he is at last, the nasty little slug!"

Four sailors were loading a boat drawn up tight against the *Louisa*'s larboard side. In the boat, two others manhandled the kegs and boxes into place. "Here you go, Davy lad," cried one of the sailors on deck, and from his voice I recognized him as Dennis O'Leary, who had a kindness for me because we both were Irish. "It's not so far a step down."

Even so, I was glad enough that O'Leary swung me down from above and someone in the boat guided my legs from below. I dropped into the boat and took my place between a keg of nails and a pouch of mail, just visible in the light of the lanterns up on deck. As the last articles were stowed, I looked across the dark bay. Two or three ships lay at anchor closer in, their stern lanterns yellow flickers in the darkness. Beyond them loomed the town of Port Royal, dark blocks of buildings with here and there a dim window lit by a candle or a lantern within.

"That's all," O'Leary shouted down. "Row dry."

Without a word, the men in the boat pushed off from the ship, and I looked back. "Mr. Bonney! Where shall I find The King's Mercy, then?"

One of the men at the oars chuckled. "At the end of a rope!" The others roared at this witticism. I sat there in the little boat, feeling abandoned. My temporary guardian had vanished, but Dennis O'Leary took pity on me.

"From the dock take the left hand turning," He called across the water. "Follow the street until you see the sign. 'Twill be on your starboard side, Davy Shea."

"And can you read the sign when you see it?" the other oarsman in the boat asked me, his tone amused.

"Sure, and I can read well enough. Mr. Horne taught me, and he a professor from Oxford and all."

"You can read?" the first boatman asked me in surprise. "How old are you?"

"Twelve. Almost twelve," I corrected, for I always told the truth, when convenient.

Both of my boat mates gave grunts of surprise at that. Not another word did they say to me until we bumped up to a pier. Then one leaped out and made the boat fast, bow and stern, and the other said, "Off you go, now, Davy Shea. Your course is larboard and bear straight until you see the sign. And the luck of the sea go with you!"

The land felt strange under my feet after so many weeks at sea. I must have staggered like a sailor who had taken more rum than his head could carry, but bearing my bundle, I walked down the pier and made my turn. All was as still and dark as it could well be. I had it in mind to ask what o'clock it was, but the boatmen were busy unloading. It had the feel of three or four in the dead of morning, though. The street about me seemed full asleep.

I walked on, the hard-packed sand of the street feeling rough beneath my bare feet. Few lights showed, and the few that did whirled about with white or pale green moths the size of my hand. The night smelled different from nights in Bristol, where my mother had reared me after my father died. I could smell the familiar fishy, salty ocean, but also something sweet and spicy. The warehouses I passed, looming out of the darkness, gave out other smells, too: dry cotton, tobacco, and molasses. Once away from the docks and the loading and unloading, everything was still and warm, and the whole place seemed less like a town and more like a great sea beast slumbering. At last I saw ahead a sign hanging over a door, and over the sign a lantern.

I had just passed an alley when I heard a growl behind me. My heart thudded into my throat, and I spun around like a leaf in a gale, nearly crouching to the earth in my alarm.

From the dark alley, a dog had crept. I could not well see him, for the hanging lantern was still fifty steps away. The beast was just a shadowy dark shape, snarling and growling at me. I could tell he was a big one, though, and I caught the white flash of his bared teeth.

"Get away!" I yelled, hoping my voice did not

show as much fear as I felt. The dog barked at me savagely, remarkably unimpressed.

I had it in mind that so unpleasant a creature probably had known rocks to be thrown at him. Quickly I stooped, grabbed a handful of air, and raised my arm back. "Go!"

Sure enough, the mongrel flinched away. I raised my arm higher, and he turned and trotted off a piece. Then he stopped and growled back over his shoulder at me. I stamped the earth and pretended to throw a stone, and the coward of a cur ran back into his alley. I turned on my heel and made good time down Thames Street, toward the next lantern.

In its light, the sign creaked back and forth in the humid breeze. I could read the words "The King's Mercy," painted in bold red letters. And dangling from the sign, as it would from a gallows, swung a hangman's noose. King James's mercy at the end of a rope. The boatman had not been just making a joke, after all.

But the lantern aside, the whole house was dark, and I hesitated to pound upon the door. It could not be long until daybreak, I told myself. So I stuffed my seabag behind me for comfort's sake, settled in the doorway, and leaned back to wait.

Saints in heaven, but I was weary. I told myself not to sleep, though. The big mongrel dog might come back. But it was probably safe just to sit quietly and rest. Closing my eyes, I thought with a pang of my poor mother. My father I could hardly remember, for he had served in the king's army and was rarely home. Up until the previous March, my whole world was the little house in Bristol, where my mother worked as a housekeeper for old Mr. Horne. I thought of him as the learned man of the world.

Mr. Horne had retired from teaching years and years before and had come to live in a small little house that his father had left him. He was spindly as a cricket, and to me he seemed a hundred years old, though I am sure he could not really have been past eighty. But he was not testy toward young people, as the old often are. He took a real interest in me, and we always spent an hour or more every day, him teaching me my letters and my numbers, and then listening to me read, or correcting what I wrote.

Mr. Horne was an old bachelor with no family to

speak of, but he treated me like a favorite grandson for all that. I do believe that he would have taken me into his family by adoption after my mother died in March, if he had not been so very ancient. Still and all, it was Mr. Horne who had found out where my doctor uncle, Patrick Shea, had gone to live, and it was he who had bought me passage and had given me a present of money on the day that we sailed for Jamaica.

Despite all the heat and all my fever at being ashore again, I shivered there, leaning against the door of the King's Mercy. My Uncle Patrick. Even the very words sounded strange. My mother had rarely spoken of her brother-in-law, and I knew nothing about him, other than he had studied medicine at Trinity College in Dublin and had qualified as a surgeon. My understanding was that he had gone off to sea at about the time my father and mother married—some disagreement had risen between the brothers Shea, I gathered, but Lord knows what its nature might have been.

And now I was to live with him here, on this strange island. A dog howled somewhere, far off. I relaxed a bit. If it was my mongrel, he was going away from me. Above me the night insects spun in a storm around the lantern. The island air seemed too warm, and the creaking sign almost like a clock ticking. My eyelids felt as if they were made of lead.

To keep myself occupied, I began to whisper a prayer for my mother's soul. After one or two repetitions, I began to jumble the words. I closed my eyes to help me better concentrate, and before I knew it, the prayer trailed off and sleep crept in, and I dropped into a dream of my mother singing an old Irish song to me.

CHAPTER TWO

I Am Robbed

NOW WHEN I NEXT opened my eyes, didn't I get the surprise of the world, though? I really felt as though I had no more than blinked, closing my eyelids on darkness—and then lifted them on sunlight, bustle, and noise!

Carts, both horse-drawn and handcarts, trundled past. Bands of men strolled and sauntered toward the docks, laughing and shoving one another. Most were barefoot and wore on their heads colorful scarves and had earrings dangling from their ears. Down the street I could see the bay, broad and gleaming in the morning light. Where in the night I had seen only three or four vessels, now dozens of ships rode at anchor or ghosted along under short sail. Gulls wheeled and screamed. For a wild moment I did not know where I was. Before I could recover my wits, someone opened the door behind me, and I, still leaning on it, tumbled backwards, a girl's piercing shriek cutting through my ears.

I scrambled to my feet and opened my mouth but before I could speak, the girl who had opened the door shrieked again and threw a pail of cold water full into my face. It went into my open mouth and up my nose, and it tasted of soap and made me cough.

"Get out of here, you dirty little beggar!" The girl shoved at me, with me trying to wipe the stinging soap from my eyes. My heel caught my seabag, and over I went, sitting down hard in the roadway and sputtering like a kettle with a loose lid.

"Watch out, there!" shouted a hoarse, angry voice. I got my burning eyes open just enough to see a mule clomping toward me, and on all fours I scuttled out of its way.

"Get away!" the girl yelled again, brandishing her wooden pail as if she wished to brain me with it.

I coughed up a bubble or two. "Wait, wait! Is—is this where Doctor Patrick Shea lives? For it is he whom I wish to see," I spluttered.

The girl glared at me suspiciously but she did lower the pail. She was my age or a bit older, a skinny thing wearing a gray dress, an apron, and a bonnet that might have been white once upon a time. Her face was plain enough, sprinkled across the nose with freckles. Her eyes were wide and brown, and some curls of brown hair escaped the bonnet at each side of her forehead. She put one hand on her hip and glowered at me. "What would the likes of you want with Doctor Shea?"

"He's my uncle," I said, trying to wring some water from my sopping shirt.

"I've never heard him mention a nephew, and I know everything about those who lodge at The King's Mercy."

"We've not been a very close family. I've only just come off the ship from England. He is my uncle, truly. He must have had a letter about me by now."

For a few seconds she stood staring at me, head to toe. "I don't know. Maybe you'd better come inside." She sniffed haughtily and stared at me down her pug nose. "You're filthy, you know."

I tried to brush mud from the knees of my breeches, but just spread it around. Picking up my seabag, I followed the girl inside, making sure I stayed out of the reach of her pail. The inn had a stone floor, and it seemed to be a fine brick building, from what I could see with my watering eyes.

"Wait here," the girl said, pushing me into a sort of cubby. "And don't touch anything, for I shall know if you do!" She left me, and as soon as I was sure she was gone, I dug out one of my other shirts, pulled off the wet one, and pulled on the dry.

In a moment, the girl had returned with a woman, plump and pleasant-looking, with a red face, her cheeks as round as apples. She was dressed just like the girl, apron, bonnet, and all. "My daughter tells me you're Doctor Patch's nephew," she said.

I must have stared at her like an idiot boy. "Doctor Patch?"

"I told you he was lying," the girl muttered under her breath.

Her mother sighed hugely, but she smiled at me. "Which we call Doctor Shea Doctor Patch here. It's a kind of nickname the sailors gave him, on account of how he patches them up."

"Doctor Patrick Shea is my uncle," I told her. "May I see him, if you please?"

"Lord, no! The doctor is an alligator if woken early. He's a crocodile, he is. He's a bear."

I was beginning to form a very strange picture in my mind of this uncle, I assure you.

"However," the woman continued, "you might wait for him in the little parlor. That ought to suit. It won't be wanted until the evening, and you'll be out from underfoot there. Oh, my name is Moll Cochran, young man, and this is my daughter Jessie."

Somehow I remembered a scrap of manners. "Pleased I am to meet you both. My name is David Shea, but people call me Davy."

"Jessie, take Davy into the little parlor."

"Mother!" Jessie exclaimed. "He's all muddy!"

"I have a change of clothes, so I do," I told them. "If there's a place where I might—?"

"Bless you, Davy Shea, change in the little parlor, with the door shut. Take him in, Jessie, take him in!"

Jessie led me down a short hall and opened a door. "In here with you." She sounded very displeased. I thanked her—for some reason, that seemed to annoy her—and she flounced out of the room, leaving me alone.

I found myself in a square little room with only two tables and eight chairs. The window was shuttered, but under it was a shelf, and on the shelf were some packs of playing cards. Understanding that I was in the inn's gaming room, I moved to the corner and put on a dry pair of breeches, trying to keep the mud from my wet ones from falling onto the floor. At a thought, I pulled on some stockings and put my feet into the shoes I had not worn since March, when my mother was buried. I ran my hands through my damp hair. I had no comb, so I smoothed it the best I could. It was never very tidy, anyway, and used to be my mother's despair.

Wrapping my muddy breeches in my damp shirt to put them back into the bag, I found the purse that the Reverend Mr. Bonney had given me. That reminded me that I was hungry. Well, the purse held five-and-twenty shillings. That was enough, I thought, to feed a king right well. While I waited for my uncle, I would have some breakfast.

I opened the door and followed the aroma of fresh-baked bread, bacon, even eggs. It led me to a room crowded with half a dozen tables, each table occupied by two or three or four men, all talking and eating at once, and Mrs. Cochran and Jessie running their legs off fetching and carrying. Jessie caught sight of me and came over frowning. "What do you want?" she demanded. "Mother said for you to wait in the little parlor!"

"Something to eat. I haven't had much more than bread and water these past weeks aboard ship. Everything smells so good," I said, making my voice very humble. "I can pay."

"It will be an egg and some bread, then, for that's all we have left. Oh, go back to the parlor and I'll fetch it to you. What have you done with your dirty clothes?"

"All wrapped up. They won't drip on the floor. I don't want to be a trouble to you at all."

"Go on. I'll be there in a minute."

So I returned to the parlor. She was there, sure enough, not a minute after me, with a pewter plate holding two slices of fried bread and two eggs. My mouth began to water just at the sight of real food. In the other hand Jessie held a pewter cup brimming with frothy white milk. "Here. This is the best we can do."

"Thank you." I opened the little cloth purse. "And how much will that be?" Shaking the coins into my hand, I looked down and felt sick.

For the things I had shaken out of the bag were not shillings at all, but iron washers. A scornful laugh burst out from Jessie Cochran. "So you're the nephew of a doctor, are you? I knew you were a cheating little beggar the second I—"

The look I gave her must have been wild, for she actually stopped talking. "I've been robbed!" Instantly I knew who had done it. "The Reverend Mr. Bonney!"

"Wait!" Jessie called, but I had already pushed past her. In a heartbeat I was in the street, running through the crowd, my bag in one hand, the worthless purse in the other. Even more exotic sights and sounds assaulted me. I almost ran down a man with half a dozen scarlet and emerald green parrots perched on his outstretched arms. Dodging and ducking, I reached the wharves. An enormous black man stood there shouting orders at some sailors in an approaching boat.

I ran up to him. "Sir! Sir! Can you tell me where is the *Louisa*, out of Bristol?"

He gave me a look of astonishment. "*Louisa*? Boy, the *Louisa* catted her anchor before daylight. She's halfway to Saint Kitts by now!"

"But she can't! She just . . . can't . . ." I broke off, for the man had turned away from me and back to his business.

I walked a few paces from him and stared across the water. A schooner had weighed anchor, and the sailors were raising the mainsail. Faintly I could hear their chant:

> "Hoist the sail and off we go,
> To the Gulf of Mexico,
> Haul, boys, haul!
> Haul, boys, haul!
> Haul, my hearties, we're away,
> There's gold in Nombre Dios Bay!
> Haul, boys, haul . . ."

Though it was useless, I wandered all the way to the end of Thames Street and stood staring out at the blue-green ocean. I had been robbed, and by a man of the cloth! Even if he was a Protestant! It scalded my heart to think of it.

How long I stood there, I don't know. But when I turned around, four boys stood shoulder to shoulder in front of me, blocking my way. They were all of them barefoot and wearing ragged clothes, and the least of them was at least half a head taller than me.

"What's in the bag?" one of them asked me.

I shook my head. "I've got to get to my uncle."

Two of the boys stepped closer together, keeping me from pushing between them. "Let us have a look." One of them reached for my bag.

I pulled back. "This is mine! All I have in the world! I'm an orphan—"

"He's an orphan, mates," one of the boys told the others. "That makes everything different." And, pivoting on his foot, he punched me in the stomach so hard, he took the wind right out of me. I felt one of the others yank the bag from my grip.

They fled, laughing like lunatics. Almost doubled over, I pelted after them, yelling in my rage. They had pulled my clothes from the seabag. One of them had my wet shirt and breeches under his arm. A second carried the black mourning suit. A third had the bag, and the last had my only other breeches, waving them like a flag.

They went four different ways. I kept after the one with my suit, the heaviest of the four, I judged. And at the corner, I threw myself forward and grabbed the thief's ankles, spilling him into the street. A horse neighed and reared, and someone swore and lashed my shoulders with a cane. It made no matter to me, so angry was I by that time. The thief, an ugly squashed-nosed bruiser, threw my clothes to the ground and came at me with raised fists.

"A fight! A fight!" someone yelled, and sure I was that the crowd was going to help me. But I was sadly mistaken in that. Instead, they gathered around us, leaving the thief and me an open space in the middle.

"A shilling on the fat boy!" someone yelled.

"Matched! Who'll go on the little one?"

"He looks Irish! I'll take him! Two shillings, says I!"

"That's more like it!" another shouted. "Hit him, Redhead!"

The heavy boy threw a blow at my head, but he was slow with it, and I ducked. Coming up, I shot two good ones at his stomach, getting a bit of my own back. He roared like a lion and threw his arms wide, trying to grab me. Again I ducked, got behind him, and gave him a stinging kick in the seat of his breeches. He turned in time for me to hit him again in the stomach, and this time he went down, bawling like a poleaxed steer.

Though I was hardly aware of anything but the fight, the crowd began to part, with shouts of warning. "Out of that, boy!" someone yelled. That distracted me.

Faster than I thought he could have done it, the fat thief leaped to his feet and threw a punch to my face, a punch that I could not block. I saw an explosion of yellow light, took a step back, and roared. In a second, I had closed with the thief and was pummeling him, stomach, chest, and sides, while he backed away, trying to draw back for another punch.

"Stop this instant, or you both will hang!"

The voice came from behind me, a great booming voice. The thief, who now had a bloody lip, turned pale as a ghost. "The governor!" he yelled, and took to his heels.

Shaky on my feet, I turned to see what the matter was. A rich-looking coach drawn by four white horses had pulled to a halt in the street, and leaning out the window of it was a man in a scarlet and gold doublet, a ruff at his throat, and a broad plumed hat on his head. A mass of curly black hair, shot with gray, spilled down on either side of his heavy face, and a mustache and beard gave him the look of a magistrate. "Out of the street, boy!" the man thundered.

I snatched up my suit, all sandy now, and backed through the crowd.

The other three were not in sight. And I was lost. The coach rattled past, and I asked a stranger, a kindly looking man, "Will you tell me the nearest way to Thames Street?"

The man laughed. "For a skinny lad, you've got nerve, I'll say that much for you. Look, d'ye know who it was in the coach that shouted you out of the street?"

I shook my head. My left eye was beginning to throb, and I was feeling sick in the pit of my stomach.

The stranger clapped me on the shoulder. "That was Sir Henry Morgan, lad. He was governor of Jamaica years ago, and though he's in disgrace with the island's council now, he still has influence. What's more, he's a pirate!"

"A pirate?" I blinked. From what I had seen, the man was middle-aged and fat, not my idea of a buccaneer at all.

"A pirate," said the stranger firmly. "With the temper of a pirate. Why, he'd as soon split you chin to belt buckle as look at you! Consider yourself fortunate."

I blinked my swelling eye. "Faith, and I would consider myself fortunate to make my way back to The King's Mercy, for it's completely lost I am."

"The King's Mercy in Thames Street?"

"Is there more than one?"

"There's little enough king's mercy anywhere—either in Whitehall in London or Thames Street in Jamaica. But take the left turning there—"

"By the tobacconist's?"

"Aye, and the next street is the one you want. Turn left, and you'll see The King's Mercy. This is a small town."

I thanked the man. Following his directions, I soon enough found my way back to the inn. Jessie met me at the door. I half-expected another face full of mop water, but one look at my bruises must have been enough to stop her. She didn't even say a word, but pointed sternly down the hall to the little parlor. The eggs and bread were cold, but I ate them, anyway. Surely my uncle would pay for my breakfast.

At least, I dearly hoped he would.

CHAPTER THREE

The Surgeon

JESSIE COCHRAN STOOD back as her mother swabbed at my bruises with a wet cloth and said, "See, Mother, the boy is just a common brawler as well as a thief!"

"Hush, Jessie. Davy Shea, your eye is a sight!"

I could well believe it. The eyelid was so swollen that I could see just through a puffy slit, and I had had black eyes enough to know that it must be as purple as a plum by that time. But instead of talking about my black eye, I just asked, "Is my uncle always this late in rising? Ow."

"Hold still or I'll never get it clean! He rises when he wants to rise," Mrs. Cochran answered me. "Don't fret yourself, Davy Shea. It ain't that he's a drunkard, nor that he games at cards. He's a good surgeon, though, and never says no to someone sick. He was with one of his patients until past two in the morning, so of course he's weary today."

"What is he like, my uncle?"

Mrs. Cochran shook her head and made a tight purse of her mouth. "I don't talk about my boarders. 'Tis a rule of mine."

"But he's my uncle." I sighed. "My father was a soldier and was never home, and he's dead now. I scarce can remember him at all, and my mother was taken three months ago. I've no one but Uncle Patrick in the world, so I have a natural curiosity about him. Ow."

With a chuckle, Mrs. Cochran said, "I said hold still, didn't I? You talk like a book. Mayhap you want to be a doctor, too, like your uncle?"

"I hardly know, since I know nothing of what kind of man he is."

At that, Mrs. Cochran laughed outright. "What a little devil you are! Yet I can see the resemblance, too. Your uncle has a flattering tongue when he pleases. It just doesn't please him much." She shook her head. "To tell you the truth, Doctor Patch is a rum sort of a man. He keeps himself to himself, and comes and goes as he pleases. Now and again he gets the itch to go to sea, and he'll come to me and say, 'Now, Mrs. Cochran, I've a three months' voyage to Jamestown and back again, so don't look to see me until then.' And he puts gold in my hand, in order that I'll keep his room just as it is. And three months later, as it may be, he walks through my door and says, 'And what will be for supper, Mrs. Cochran?' Just as if he'd been gone for hours instead of weeks."

"Is he"—I thought of how to put it—"is he a kind man?"

"Kind?" She tilted her head thoughtfully to one side. "Well, well, his tongue can have an edge to it, and always in the mornings he's apt to fly out at a body. But if a sick person is poor, why, he'll ask never a fee of them, but give them medicines for free. And when he's got a long-standing case, like Lieutenant Hunter, nobody could be more obliging than Doctor Patch."

"Who's Lieutenant Hunter? Ow."

Mrs. Cochran gave a glance toward the ceiling, as

if the lieutenant were hanging there like a chandelier. "Ah, poor soul, he was third mate on the king's ship *Brilliant*. They chased Jack Steele, the terrible pirate, last month, and Steele's ship got in a wicked broadside that swept the *Brilliant*'s deck. Killed twenty men outright, so they say, and wounded dozens more."

For the moment I forgot all about the pain in my eye. "Did they take the pirate?"

"They did not. He got clean away, leaving the *Brilliant* as bloody as a shambles. Lieutenant Hunter, he was pierced through and through by a dreadful long splinter, so they thought he'd never live. But the *Brilliant* limped to port here, and they brought the man to the inn on a shutter, and Doctor Patch took one look at him and said, 'I can save him if we're quick about it.'"

"And did he?"

Mrs. Cochran started to speak but it was Jessie who took up the tale with more animation than I had ever seen. "Oh, it was terrible! They brought Mr. Hunter into the parlor, shoved those very tables together, and there he lay while Doctor Patch cut and sewed and stitched, and the poor fellow that white with loss of blood and it spurting all over the place!"

"But save him your uncle did," said Mrs. Cochran in a firm voice as she stared pointedly at her daughter. Jessie lowered her head and glared at me as if her outburst was my fault. Her mother smiled at me and continued. "And now the lieutenant is just beginning to be able to stir about again. Is your uncle kind? I'll warrant the lieutenant thinks he is, seeing that Doctor Patch saved his life. There! That's the best I can do. Come, Jessie, while we're in a cleaning mood, there's a whole common room as could use it."

They left me again at that. I took some heart, however, from their story. Surely, I thought, any doctor must have a tender heart. I sat back and waited some more.

Mrs. Cochran had left the door open, and looking out into the hall, I saw people passing to and fro. To my eyes, they were strange and foreign: Men with deep brown tans, men with tattoos on their arms, men who swaggered with swords at their sides and whose voices rolled through the house like the echoes of distant gunfire. Hours crept by, and all the while I sat waiting, with nothing to distract me but my aching eye and my skinned knuckles.

Jessie passed by once, looked in and saw me, and said, "What is Mother thinking? People will see you sitting there all bloody and lose their appetites. You're a disgrace upon the house!" I had hoped she was about to offer me soap and water. Instead, she closed the door upon me again and all I could hear were her angry footsteps stamping back to the common room.

Left alone, I leaned forward and rested my head on one of the small tables. Would Uncle Patrick never stir? Sitting there, I was torn between hope of seeing him and a rising feeling of resentment that he should leave me here for so long without even having the consideration to wake up and come and give me a good morning. The fact that he probably didn't even know I was there never entered my head. It would likely be a good evening by the time he appeared, I thought.

At long last, just as I was beginning to despair of ever seeing my uncle at all, I heard footsteps on the stair, a rumble of voices, and then the door to the little parlor opened. "Here he is," said Mrs. Cochran.

A tall, broad-shouldered man stepped through the doorway. He looked shabby. His red hair was pulled back into a ponytail. A growth of whiskers bristled on his thin cheeks, like a brush made of coppery wires. He had a great hawk's beak of a nose, scowling eyebrows, and green eyes with bloodshot whites to them. "Nephew?" he said in a loud, irritable voice. "Nephew? This boy with the black eye and the runny nose? What nonsense is this, then?"

I stood up and took a deep breath, smelling the aromas of rum and food, odors that seemed soaked into the very walls of The King's Mercy. As well as I could, I made a polite bow. "If you're Doctor Patrick Shea, then I'm your nephew David, come to you from Bristol. Sir, my mother is dead. Mr. Horne told me he'd written to you."

Those strange green eyes looked stunned. "Kathleen—dead? How? When?"

I lowered my head. "Smallpox, sir. It took her on the thirteenth of March. It must have been in the letter."

My uncle blinked, then he swallowed hard. "No, I've had no word at all. Sure, the letter must have miscarried. Kathleen Sullivan, the beauty of the world, dead!" He crossed himself. "Rest her soul."

"And I've come to live with you, sir."

Instantly, his expression grew hard. "Oh, no. Oh, no, no, no. I'd have the devil of a life with a youngster at my heels, always hungry and no doubt as ignorant as dirt—"

And at that, I boiled over. I could not help it, with all that had happened since the Reverend Mr. Bonney had wakened me that day. I shouted, "All right, then! If that's your word, then so be it! I'll make my own way in the world, so I shall! Shut of me you will be, for I'd not spend a night under any roof of yours, no, not if you begged me to do it!"

He blinked those green eyes, and surprise flew into them. "You insolent little pup! You ought to have a strap taken to your breech, to pound some manners into your skin!"

I ran past him and had almost reached the front door when he reached me—he ran as silently as a cat, and I heard never a sound of footsteps. He grabbed my shoulders and spun me around. "Stop it now! Run out into a strange town, and you hurt? Are you crazy?" He glared at me in some alarm. "Here, you're not about to cry, are you?"

Tears stood in my eyes, but they were tears of fury. I jerked but could not free myself from his grip, for his hands were powerful. "And if I am, who has better cause?"

He frowned at me. "And what's the cause? That bruise? Did you try to pick an honest man's pocket and get cuffed for your insolence? What happened?"

Rage burned hot within me. "What happened? What happened! Why, I've been left an orphan, and sent halfway round the world, and robbed by a minister, and nearly eaten by a dog the size of a calf, and half-drowned by a snotty freckly girl, and beaten by four boys twice as big as I am, and robbed of all but the clothes I stand in and the suit I wore to see my mother buried! And then kept waiting and waiting in my pain and grief until my slug-a-bed uncle crept out of his cot! That's what happened!"

"Here, don't cry now," he said, sounding really alarmed.

"I have reason enough!" I repeated. "But you'll have no tears from me, Uncle, no, not if one drop of a tear would save your sorry soul from a thousand years of torment in Purgatory, you won't!"

"Won't I, though, now?" my uncle bellowed. "What a wicked thing to say! Now, see here—"

"Oh, whisht! You've nothing to say that I want to hear, you stony-hearted villain. Let me go!"

"And you think you're man enough to make a living in Port Royal, do you?"

"Live or die, what's it to you? You owe these people for eggs and butter that I ate, until I can find some way to earn the money to pay ye back. My father was Gerald Shea, my mother was Kathleen Sullivan Shea, and I'm David Michael Shea, and that ought to be enough for ye to find me in a place as small as Port Royal, and—and I don't know if you're truly my uncle or not, but to the devil with ye, anyway!"

I would have left him standing there, but he still held my shoulders and would not let me go. A rueful smile broke out on his unshaven face. "Well, you've got the temper of the Sheas, right enough." And then, more quietly: "And sure, you've got

Kathleen's hazel eyes. And you tell me sweet Kathleen Sullivan is dead, the pity and the sorrow." To my shock, he ran an absent hand through my hair. "We must light a candle for her soul's rest. So we must, for the two of us, well, we're the last of the Sheas now." He shook his head and then raised his voice. "Mrs. Cochran! The little lumber room next to mine—could you move a bed in there, if I bought one?"

"Today, Doctor Patch," she said from behind him. "Now, if you like—Jessie!"

Oh, she's surely going to love that bit of news, I thought, feeling rather than seeing her sullen gaze hot on the back of my neck.

"No, I don't much like it," my uncle confessed to Mrs. Cochran. "I don't much like it at all. To have David Michael Shea show up just at this time and just in this place—no, I have reasons of my own for not liking it."

"No more do I," I told him.

He did that strange stroke through my hair again. "But if this young powdersack can stomach me as an uncle, I suppose I can try to stomach him as a nephew. Truce?"

"You don't have to do a thing for me," I insisted. "I can do without you."

"Maybe you can, and maybe you cannot. But Sheas we both are, and as Sheas I think we two should stand against the world. Will you be still and listen, now, if I let go of you?"

I stood breathing hard. At last I nodded, and he dropped his hands from my shoulders.

"Very well," he said, and he drew himself up. "Nephew, I am Doctor Patrick Gabriel Shea, bachelor of medicine, Trinity College, Dublin, currently practicing at the sign of The King's Mercy, Port Royal, Jamaica. People in general call me Patch."

He held out his hand. I shook it, the fire of my anger replaced by a dull, bleak ache within my chest. "And I'm David Michael Shea, your nephew. People always call me Davy."

In a grave and, yes, kindly voice, he said, "Welcome home, Davy."

Sure, and it's strange how the feelings work. I was fine until he said that word "home." And then, despite all I could do to hold them back, the tears came at last, and they rolled down my face.

And that strange, towering man embraced me in a rough and awkward hug and just like that, I was home.

CHAPTER FOUR

Patients

AS I WRITE, I try to look back on the rest of that Friday in June 1687, but nothing at all do I remember of it. My uncle must have been as good as his word, for I do recall that night I slept in my own bed in the room next to his. Strange it was at first, for I had become used to the motion of a ship, and to sleep in a bed that did not roll and rise and fall was now hard for me to do.

Mine was a small room, five steps deep and five steps across, I suppose, and the ceiling of it slanted so that the outer wall was but chest high, and to get into my bed, I had to stoop. Still I had my own window in a dormer, and the air that came through might have been hot, but it was clean and fresh and had none of the stink of between-decks.

And, sure, I suppose that we must have bespoke some clothes for me that afternoon, because the next morning when I got up, they were folded neat in the locker at the foot of my bed. To me they seemed rich: black shoes with silver buckles, white stockings, knee-length brown breeches, a white ruffled shirt, a black vest, and a light brown jacket. Even at my mother's funeral I had never worn such finery.

I had just finished dressing when there was a heavy pounding on my door. A moment later, my uncle bawled out, "David Michael Shea, are ye decent? Mrs. Cochran's breakfasts are plentiful but they wait for no man and when they're gone, they're gone!"

I opened the door and hurried after his retreating footsteps. The sun was well up, but I had the feeling that Uncle Patrick had made a special effort to rise early, or at least early for him.

We sat at one of the tables below stairs, and Mrs. Cochran herself brought fried fish, hot bread, cheese, butter, clotted cream, and strange tropical fruits to us. I had never seen a mango, no, nor an orange, in the whole of my life before, and to me they were like the food the angels must eat in Paradise. The girl Jessie brought my uncle mug after mug of steaming black coffee, but never a glance did she give me, and never a compliment on how well I must have looked in my new suit.

My uncle shook his head as he looked at me. He had shaved, and he had made some effort to tidy himself up, but still any clothes he put on fell to wrinkles at once on him. "Your eye is still badly swollen," he said. "Clap your hand over your good one."

Still munching an orange, I put my right hand over my right eye.

"Can you see clear?" Uncle Patrick asked.

I nodded, my mouth full and juice dribbling down my chin.

"Look at the window. Do you see rays shooting out of the light? Does it look cloudy?"

I shook my head.

"Maybe you'll keep the sight in it, then. Now what are we to do with you?"

Finally swallowing, I said, "Mrs. Cochran

thought I might train up as a surgeon, like yourself."

"Oh, she thought so, did she? If you had some Latin, now, that might—"

Instantly I said in Latin, "I speak the language, sir. What would you have me say?"

My uncle's jaw dropped so fast, I thought it would hit the table. "And where did you learn that?"

"Mr. Horne taught me, sir." I explained about him, and how he had taken an interest in my education.

"*Amo, amas, amat,* I suppose," Uncle Patrick grumbled. "Poetry and such. Listen to this." And quick as a wink, he fired off five Latin terms at me: "*Caput! Febricula! Iecur! Ossium compages! Gravedo!* Now what do you make of them?"

In English, I said, "Skull, fever, liver, and the other two I don't know, but one of them has something to do with bones."

He made an odd creaking sound, which I was to learn was his closest approach to laughter. "Well, well, well. *Ossium compages* is skeleton—there's your bones—and *gravedo* is a cold in the head.

Perhaps we'll try you out. I must make some rounds today, Nephew Davy. You shall come with me and see the kind of patients I deal with. Then maybe we shall speak more of your becoming a surgeon."

We began with the sun still rising toward noon, and a long day we had of it. I learned that Port Royal was on a narrow spit of land, shaped something like an arrowhead pointing off to the east. It was fairly packed with forts, for the town protected the whole British colony of Jamaica from the pirates and the Spanish.

Across the blue bay from Port Royal lay another little settlement, and the bay itself was alive with large and small craft. My uncle attended a merchant on Queen Street by the name of Morrow, suffering from a wicked cruel abscess on his thigh that had to be lanced and drained, him rumbling on about bills of lading and arrival dates and tonnage. We visited a building in Lime Street where half a dozen sailors lay sweltering. At first I thought they must be dying, for their eyes lacked all interest, and their breathing was slow and labored. One of them, a huge bald man, reached two fingers into his mouth and plucked out a tooth by its bloody roots as easily as I might pick a cherry from a tree, muttering, "Rotting alive, we are here."

"Nonsense," Uncle Patrick told him. "I know well what ails you, Seaman Duncan, and sure, 'tis one of the diseases for which there is a quick and pleasant cure." He turned to me and added, "Davy, these men are all suffering from the scurvy. Some of you have old wounds? You? Yes, and it has opened again, has it not? 'Tis a sure sign of the disease, Nephew, when old scars bleed fresh. Scurvy then, you may bet your teeth on it. But we'll have these six on their feet again in no time. All it takes is a diet with fresh green vegetables." Here there were many loud and theatrical groans, for as I was to learn, sailors were fast attached to their diets of salt beef, salt pork, and cheese. "And above all, the juice of lemons, drunk faithfully morning, noon, and night."

"Can we cut it with rum?" one of the other sailors called out to general laughter.

"Aye, that ye may, and then ye'll give me even

more business! By next week you'll all have forgotten that ever you were sick!"

After that, we saw women who were expecting babies, and an old gentleman afflicted with gout in his swollen left foot, and three or four cases of tropical fevers. I tried to keep their names straight, but it was beyond me. Uncle Patrick, however, not only knew their names but all their kin and all of their kins' ailments.

At a private house in High Street, to my surprise, I saw the man who had shouted at me from his carriage, Sir Henry Morgan. He was resting in a chair, with his feet propped up. My uncle greeted him with a cheery, "Good day to you, now, Sir Henry."

"And what's good about it, says I?" Sir Henry grunted irritably. Though he was dressed well in a dark plum-colored suit and white stockings, he seemed less a gentleman than a brawler dressed in his Sunday best. He scowled darkly at me and said, "I saw this young swab fighting in the streets. What have you done, bought him as a slave to carry your instruments?"

"The devil I have," returned Uncle Patrick. "Sir Henry Morgan, pray allow me to introduce my nephew David, come here to live with me."

"To live with you?" Morgan asked. He gave my uncle a meaningful look. "To live, d'ye say?"

"Don't fret yourself, now, Sir Henry. These things have a way of working themselves out, you know. How do you feel today, then?"

"Fat and old and short of breath," snapped Sir Henry.

"Faith, you're not so old, though your tonnage has run up these past years. As for being short of breath, why I've told you and told you that you have a dropsical tendency, and 'twould be far better for you to eat more sparingly and to give up the rum entirely."

Morgan grunted and waved his hand, as though my uncle's advice were a cloud of annoying flies. "Did you hear the council is petitioning for my reinstatement again?" he asked.

Uncle Patrick was pressing his fingers against Sir Henry's belly. "I don't like the feel of your liver at all. Hear that the council wants to reinstate you? No, not I."

"Careful, blast your eyes! You're not plumping a pillow, you Irish blackguard! They want me to take my seat again as a member of the government. If our slave-trading idiot of an acting governor, Hender Molesworth, had an ounce of brains in his head, he would listen to them. Lord knows it would help his chances of staying in office. With Jack Steele loose in the islands and Tortuga giving pirates safe haven, they need me."

"Perhaps they do, too. Now, Sir Henry, be so good as to show me the color of your tongue."

I have to say that I stared in an ill-mannered way at Morgan. Even in our quiet corner of England I had heard tales of this buccaneer king. In his day, he had thumped the Spanish again and again, taking Portobello, invading Maracaibo, and proving himself the terror of the Spanish Main. I wondered what he had looked like in his prime, for certainly now he did not seem to be a dangerous man, but rather a heavy, slow, and sick one. He groaned in pain when my uncle again pressed on his stomach, and he finally consented in the meekest way to take his medicines.

As I watched Uncle Patrick deftly examine the former governor of Jamaica, I began to think that a surgeon's way of life might be just what I would like. People everywhere greeted my uncle civilly, he seemed to be highly respected, and when he had even an important patient, like Sir Henry, he could order them about with great confidence. Of course, at that time I thought Uncle Patrick was simply a surgeon and nothing else. Little did I know he had another side to him—but that will come later, in its own place.

For now, I will say that by the time we walked toward The King's Mercy, the afternoon was well advanced. Shadows had grown long, and the air hummed with heat and with the droning of insects and the chatter of strange, bright-colored birds.

"What did you think of His Excellency, Sir Henry?" asked Uncle Patrick as we passed by The Goat and Compass, a noisy tavern where sailors shouted for drink and sang drunken songs.

"He seemed a man of temper," I answered.

My uncle creaked out a short laugh. We crossed the street between two trundling carriages loaded with barrels of beer or rum. "Aye, he is that," he agreed. "Touchy as a serpent with a toothache!"

"Yet he was a great privateer, was he not?"

My uncle gave me a keen glance from his green eyes. "Faith, some say so."

"But not you?"

We turned onto Thames Street. Uncle Patrick shook his head. "Truth to tell, Davy lad, Sir Henry Morgan may have been the worst captain ever to hoist anchor. Rare was the time he returned to Port Royal aboard the same ship he had set out in! More often than not, the one he had sailed in had been sunk from under him."

"But I thought—"

He waved aside my thought. "Mark you, I am not saying he was a bad fighter. Far from it! Onshore, Morgan was a terror and a scourge to the Spanish. But his true strength was as a soldier, not as a sailor. His greatest victories came after he landed troops and led them against Spanish forts, not on the open sea."

Despite myself, I yawned. "It has been a long day," I murmured apologetically.

"We're not finished yet," my uncle warned me. "One last patient, and a particular friend of mine. His name is Lieutenant William Hunter, and he was cruelly wounded at sea not very long ago."

Mrs. Cochran met us at the door with the brightest smile and the word that the brave young lieutenant—for so she called him—had come downstairs and was in the little parlor, the same place where I had been kept waiting. Jessie, standing behind her mother, looked at me as if I were a toad or a loathsome insect, but she said nothing. I supposed her mother had warned her to be civil, or perhaps she was shy before my uncle.

We walked into the small parlor to find our patient half-reclining in a chair. He was a thin young man with blue eyes, and blond hair worn in a queue, in the way of sailors. His face was gaunt, with hollow cheeks and a sunken look, and his complexion was a strange yellowish color, as if beneath its surface tan it had turned as pale as parchment. "Doctor," he said as my uncle stepped in, "you see I have made it belowdecks at last!"

"I see that you have disobeyed my orders not to stir until I said you might. However, let me feel your pulse, and then I want a look at your scars."

Uncle Patrick took from his pocket a very fine-looking silver watch. He consulted it as he took the young man's pulse. "Not so very bad," he pronounced at last. "Steady and stronger, at any rate, than it has been. Well, Lieutenant William Hunter, allow me to present my nephew, David Shea. He is not, as you might suppose from his purple eye, a mere ruffian, but a young fellow of some brain. Open your shirt, sir."

This last was not said to me, but to Lieutenant Hunter. Slowly, as if the effort was a strain on him, but with evident good temper, the man undid and opened his shirt. He wore a great bandage underneath, wound around and around him. When my uncle loosened this, I gasped despite myself at what I saw.

From his right shoulder down his side to the bottom of his ribs, a great jagged, puckered pink scar ran. The marks of stitches were plain, though the stitches themselves were gone. It was a terrible cruel wound, and looking at it I had to wonder how Lieutenant Hunter could have survived it. My uncle carelessly dropped the bandages, and on them I could see a few brown traces of blood.

Uncle Patrick pressed the scar here and there. Most of it had healed over, but in one or two spots some bloody fluid still oozed. Uncle Patrick sniffed the air as if he were a hunting dog. "I congratulate you, sir. No smell of gangrene, the saints be praised. Now your leg, if you please."

With a wry look at me, as though to say, "You see how I am ordered about," Mr. Hunter further undressed, down to his underclothing. He had another wound in his right thigh, or rather two wounds, one of them four inches long, a wicked curved C of a scar, and the other only about an inch. "Very good," my uncle murmured. "David, could you guess what caused these?"

"A splinter?" It was not that much of a guess, for I had heard Mrs. Cochran mention it.

"A splinter indeed! Full marks, young Doctor Davy!" Hunter agreed. "A sharp and thin one, at that. It went in here"—he pointed to the larger wound on the outside of his thigh—"and part of it came out through here." This was the smaller one, somewhat lower and much paler, on the inside. "Fortunately, or so Doctor Patch here tells me, it only grazed the bone."

"It must have been terribly painful, sir," I observed.

"It was, rather. The gash on my chest was, I think, the result of a block falling and catching me awkwardly. It was much gaudier, but not as dangerous as the leg wound, I am told."

"Both together well nigh did for you," said my uncle. "I'd bet my teeth you had hardly a quart of blood left in you by the time your ship returned to port. I'll change your dressings, and then you can get yourself decently clothed again. Have you been eating and drinking as I prescribed?"

"Faithfully. I could do with a beefsteak, though."

"So could I, if it comes to that. I think Mrs. Cochran can arrange for us both to venture that far," replied Uncle Patrick, winding a bandage around and around the leg wound. "But all the same, keep drinking your port, and all the barley-water you can stomach. You still have not enough blood in your veins, and I am far from satisfied with the state of your humors."

"Actually, there are those who consider me rather amusing."

Uncle Patrick snorted and began to bandage the great scar on Mr. Hunter's chest. I took the opportunity to beg the young naval officer's pardon and asked, "Could you tell me about the action in which you were wounded, sir?"

"Oh, aye," agreed Hunter easily. "Though there's no glory in it for me. First, let me say I was third on His Majesty's frigate *Brilliant*. We carried twenty-four guns, nine-pounders—you know what that is, young David?"

"A cannon that fires a nine-pound ball," I answered.

"Just so. Well, Jack Steele had lately taken three or four merchant ships between Florida and Hispaniola, and so we were sailing there to see if we could intercept him. We came upon him much sooner than we expected, not a hundred miles from Port Royal, before we were fairly into the Windward Passage. Steele's great ship the *Red Queen* came out of a squall only three miles off our bow, and the captain instantly had us beat to quarters."

I knew that he meant the *Brilliant* was making ready for battle. In my imagination, I saw them: the *Brilliant*, a slender, fast frigate, with three masts all square-rigged. Flying down fast on her, the *Red Queen*, which I pictured as a grim ship painted all scarlet and bristling with guns. Some of the men would be hunched over the cannons, getting them ready. Others would be aloft, up in the rigging, adjusting the sails to get the best speed from the ships.

As if he read my thoughts, Mr. Hunter said, "Aye, the *Red Queen* bore right down on us, coming on fast and throwing up a great white bow wave. We just had time to get ready, load the guns, and run them out. I was in charge of two gun crews on the starboard side, and for a few seconds I thought we had a fair chance of getting off a shot. But before we had any hope of hitting his ship, Steele put her about—his sailors are amazingly quick, as handy as navy men. The *Red Queen* turned sharp, rolling away from us as she did. And in turning, she gave us one broadside, one only. She carries sixty guns, all sixteen-pounders. Where we could throw 108 pounds of iron at her in a broadside, she could throw 480 at us, do you see?"

I could just imagine the red ship vanishing behind a billow of white smoke, could almost hear the shattering roar of the guns, the whistle of cannonballs flying overhead. I licked my lips and asked, "And he hit you?"

Mr. Hunter grimaced. "He hit the *Brilliant*, and

hammered her hard. I saw three men killed out-right. The broadside brought down the top yards of the mizzenmast and cut the foremast in half just below the top. It was a block from the foretop that did for me, and a splinter from the rail. We got off never a shot, and with the masts so mauled, we could not make sail and follow the *Red Queen*. Steele had no interest in sinking us or boarding us, seemingly. After that broadside, he sailed past us as if we were of no importance. And he was right, just at that moment. We were of no value whatever as a fighting ship. I assume his holds were full of plunder from the ships he had taken, or he might have given us more attention than he did. Are you finished, Patch?"

"It's entirely finished I am," said my uncle. "Now go and have a glass of port, and I'll see if Mrs. Cochran can cook you up a beefsteak for your supper."

Hunter rose, dressed with slow deliberation, and walked out, his steps deliberate and stiff. My uncle sank into the chair he had left with a sigh that puffed out his cheeks. "You see how it is, Davy. This town has a dozen surgeons, but I'm the best of the lot, and the result is that I'm run ragged. Well, tomorrow is Sunday, the day of rest, and that's a blessing." He stopped and looked thoughtful. Then he gave me a long, considering look. "And how long is it, now, since you've been to confession?"

The question took me by surprise. "Why, just before my mother's funeral," I said.

"What! The shame of the world!"

"Uncle," I protested, "Catholics have to be careful in England!" Indeed we did, for not that long ago our religion had been outlawed, though it was whispered that King James might be more kindly inclined toward us—might, indeed, be one of us. "I had small occasion ever to see a priest."

Uncle Patrick shook his head in a dissatisfied way. "And how often did you see one, then?"

I sighed. "Mister Horne was Catholic. He had a priest in once a month or so, usually Father Sims, and the priest always heard Mother's and my confession."

"And said Mass?"

"And said Mass in the dining room," I told him. "That being the biggest room Mister Horne had, for some few of the neighbors always came, too."

"You'll find there's no shortage of priests at all in Port Royal," said my uncle. "'Tis one advantage of living here—nobody cares what church you go to, or whether you go to one at all, for that matter. To see a priest only once a month! It's a shame on the name of Shea, that's what it is," he said decisively. "And to let months pass between confessions—"

His scolding tone began to make me feel picked on. "And how long has it been since you've been to confession yourself, Uncle Patrick?" I asked.

He glared at me for a good long minute. His cheeks grew red—from anger, I supposed. And his green eyes fairly glittered at me. "That is an impertinent question!"

"Aye, so it is," I admitted. "But how long has it been, Uncle?"

With a kind of snarl, Uncle Patrick brought his hand down flat on the table, making a crash that sounded like a gunshot. "You are going to be a trial to me, I can tell that already. Very well, you little heathen, I'll go if you will."

"Agreed," I said. Though I did not know it at the time, that was one of the few things we were to agree on for the whole rest of that summer.

CHAPTER FIVE

The Old Buccaneer

FOR THE NEXT DAYS and the next weeks, my uncle led me a sad life of it. Hours I spent poring over books, books, books, all kinds of books. Some were medical, and Uncle Patrick expected me to memorize these.

"This is Fabricius's book on anatomy, and a pretty penny it cost me, so treat it with respect. John Gerald's book of herbs and Bartholin's text on the lymph were used books and cheaper, but respect them, anyway."

"Yes, Uncle Patrick," I said with a sigh as he dropped another stack of books on the table in front of me.

"Ficini's Latin translation of Plato is fairly good. 'Tis a shame we don't have Plato in the original Greek, but you don't understand Greek, do you? More's the pity. Geoffrey of Monmouth for the humor of it. Thomas Aquinas for the good sense of it. . . ."

"Yes, Uncle Patrick."

"Lilye's *Grammar*—'tis not enough to speak the King's English, you have to be able to write it."

"Yes, Uncle Patrick."

"Don't be so agreeable, lad, for you're fooling only yourself." He placed a final pile of books on top of the others. "And the mathematics, of course."

I opened the first of the mathematics texts. It was battered and smudged and obviously well read. "Will you be helping me with any of this, Uncle Patrick?"

He gave me a stern look. "There are things a man needs to learn by himself, Davy my lad. Mathematics, now, is a personal science, a lonely taskmaster."

"Don't tease him so, Doctor Patch," muttered Mrs. Cochran as she cleared away the breakfast dishes. "Why not just tell the boy the truth?"

"The truth, Mrs. Cochran?" he asked with a touch of coldness.

"Aye, the truth, Doctor Patch." She turned to me with her hands somehow holding on to six pewter mugs at once. "Your uncle is one of the most respected surgeons in Jamaica, Davy, but, bless him, he can't add three figures and get the same answer twice."

My uncle had the good grace to laugh.

On some days he allowed me to go on his rounds with him, and these were the days I liked best. Port Royal was a brawling town, a fighting town, and a lively town. Rare was the day when we didn't spy two sailors fighting bare-knuckle in the streets ("More work for me," my uncle would observe calmly), or hear the cannons roar as one or another of the forts fired a salute to an approaching navy craft ("A lot more work for me," he would say). Most days, though, he abandoned me to the books in The King's Mercy. It was so hot during the day that I could not bear to stay in my little room beneath the eaves, but Jessie Cochran was sure to make my life a misery if I dared to come downstairs. She always had some biting remark about me being a ruffian and a villain. I don't know why, for I no longer looked like one. I took great pains with my appearance, and my black eye had faded clean away.

Many was the time her taunts moved me to anger, and I would have snapped out at her, except that I knew that if I did, she would be sure to tell her mother. Worse, she would be sure to tell my uncle, who had small patience with what he called "childish quarrels."

Once, I recall, I had taken a chair outside of the inn, for the day was broiling, and I had found a spot of shade that caught some of the breeze from the ocean. I was deep into a book on tropical fevers when I became aware that Jessie was standing hard by, frowning at me.

I closed the book, but kept my thumb between the pages to mark my place. "And what is it, then?"

"Nothing," she snapped at me. "Only I wondered where that chair had run off to!"

"Sure, and it ran nowhere, though it has four good legs," I told her.

"Don't laugh at me! I'm not stupid, you know!"

"Then don't say stupid things."

She stood there, her fists on her hips, and promptly changed the subject, something she did every time she looked to lose an argument. "What are you doing out here, anyway?"

I held up the book. "Reading."

"Always reading! I don't know what you see in it!"

"It's what my uncle told me to do," I said. I expected her to go away, but she did not. To make it clear that I had no wish for her company, I opened the book and buried my nose in it once more. But I could still feel her standing there.

"Is it hard?" she asked me in her argumentative voice.

I did not look up. "Is what hard?"

"Reading."

She said the word so quickly that she startled me. I looked up from the book and was surprised to see that she had tears standing in her eyes. "Why, can't you read?" I asked her.

She shook her head. "Why should I? I'm just an ignorant kitchen girl."

"Well, I'll not argue that. But reading isn't that hard. You could learn."

"And who would teach the likes of me?" she demanded.

"Faith, is there not a schoolmaster about?"

"None that would take girls," she said with contempt.

I thought about that for a while. "Do you not even know your ABCs?"

"I can tell some of the letters," she said. She pointed at the sign hanging in front of the inn. "There's a K, standing on two feet and holding a sword. An I, with a little round head." She frowned in concentration and stammered, "A—and an M? Or is it N? I mix them up."

"It's an N," I said, and read through the sign for her. "M begins the word 'mercy', there."

"Why do the G and the Y have tails?" she asked.

"That I do not know. 'Tis just that they have them. Born with them they were, like cats and dogs, that's all." I was struck with a sudden inspiration. "Is there a slate about, and some chalk?"

"Mother keeps one to score off the drink orders of an evening."

"Think you could get it?"

She stuck her tongue out at me, turned, and

flounced back into the inn. I thought I was free of her, but she was back almost immediately, clutching a slate larger than the largest of my books. It had been wiped, but I could see the ghosts of scores on it: no words, just long lines of straight marks counting off the glasses of rum served out.

I chalked the alphabet on it as far as M, leaving spaces. Then I handed it back to her. "Say these with me," I told her. We went through it four or five times, until Jessie knew the letters by heart. "Now, you take this and practice making your letters," I told her. "Do it for a few minutes every day. When you've got them all down well, we'll finish it up and then I'll teach you some words."

"I'd like to write my name."

"Then that'll be your first lesson."

I don't know why I thought that would keep her out of my sight. From that day on, for half an hour or so every day, we had lessons. Sure I was that the girl would get tired of trying to learn and find reading too dull and hard and give it up, but I was wrong. She stuck to her task with a tight-lipped determination. And she was much nicer to me when we were alone, though she still looked down her nose at me in public. When the day came that she slowly wrote out J-e-s-s-i-e C-o-c-h-r-a-n, I thought she would dance about in her joy at doing that simple thing. But that evening at supper, she was just as short-tempered as always.

Some days were good, and some were bad. Perhaps the worst was the morning when my uncle had been summoned by a messenger to stir himself and hurry to a woman who was about to have a baby. I rose to help him get dressed since he was in too great a hurry to do it properly, and then saw him down to the door so that I could lock it back behind him after he had left. Day was just dawning, the streets full of thin mist and a dim gray light. The lantern over The King's Mercy sign glowed, weak and yellow.

From the mist came a harsh command: "In line, curse your worthless hides, stay in line!"

To my shock, the street before the inn was full of marching men and women. They were mostly naked, they were black, and they trudged along like doomed souls, to the clank of chains. I stood there amazed until Uncle Patrick yanked me back into the doorway. They were an appalling sight, like walking skeletons, their arms and legs thin as matchsticks. Some bore the bloody marks of whips on their backs. I can never forget that one of them, a girl no older than myself, looked up dully as she passed, her gaze locking with my own. My heart leaped into my throat at the despairing expression on her face. It was the look of someone longing to die and be free of her misery.

The rough English voice yelled, "Get along there! Curse you, stay in line!" A whip cracked in the darkness, and I closed my eyes. When I opened them again, the girl had vanished in the fog, but the horrible parade still passed by. White men with muskets and uncoiled whips herded the poor wretches along. "Uncle!" I cried aloud.

He put a hand on my shoulder. "Slaves for the plantations," he said in a quiet and furious voice. "Slaves, Davy."

We watched the last of the ghastly procession disappear into the mist. "Why does God permit this?" I asked.

The hand on my shoulder gave me a reassuring pat. "I think it takes the Irish to know what loss of liberty truly means. The day will come when slavery will be ended, Davy. You may depend upon that. I only pray we live to see it." He had to rush away to his patient, but all the rest of that day my spirits were bleak and my heart torn.

So the days rolled by, the bad ones and the good, until July was well nigh gone. By that time, Lieutenant William Hunter was quite another man. He was well healed of his wounds, and he exercised every day, walking for hours. Sometimes after dinner, he and my uncle would go into a yard behind the inn, where a few chickens complained of the tropical heat, and practice at singlestick.

"Come, Patch, and see how a gentleman fights!"

"Faith, and where are you going to find one at this time of day?" my uncle snapped back.

I loved to watch these mock duels. The sticks flashed and clacked, and I often imagined the two of them fighting for real, swinging cutlasses on the deck of an embattled ship. What surprised me the most was that my uncle gave a good account of himself. Never had I thought of him as any kind of fighter.

But best of all were the days when my uncle allowed me to go with him to visit Governor

Morgan. He brought the old buccaneer relief that the other doctors in town could not. I saw my first bleeding in Morgan's room, my uncle using a sharp lancet to open a vein in the man's arm. The dark red blood streamed out into a copper basin, and I began to feel sick.

Morgan scarcely paid attention to the flow of blood, but he must have noticed my green face. "Come, come, young Davy," he said in a jolly tone. "This is nothing! Why, I've seen the day when the deck of a ship has been running red with blood. There was the time we marched to sack Panama—"

And he was off into a tale of his buccaneer days. He said that for years he had wanted to take Panama, ever since his men had raided Portobello in 1668. "The governor of that town was the bravest man I ever saw," he told me. "By the blessed Powers, if he had another dozen with his spirit, he could have fought us off! I remember he stood against a wall, wounded in a dozen places, and I called the men back. I offered him his life and his freedom, and he cursed me in Spanish and told me to meet him face-to-face. Why, I had the man's wife come and beg him to surrender, but he brandished his sword and roared at us. Ordering a man to shoot him was the hardest thing I ever had to do."

I blinked at him. He shook his head sadly. "The people of Portobello sent word to Panama for aid, but Governor de Guzman returned jests and insults instead of soldiers until it was far too late. The peacock asked me for a pattern of the weapons four hundred men had used to take a great city, and I sent him back a homely British pistol, with word that I would collect it later. Thunder! That was when I resolved that we had to visit Panama. A cruel, hard march it would be, and first the fort at Castillo San Lorenzo had to fall. For that I dispatched my right-hand man, Joseph Bradley. He was a soldier and no mistake. With him went four hundred picked men."

"That's a pint," observed my uncle, and he took the copper basin from my hands. "Now let me bandage this."

Morgan seemed lost in the past. "The Castillo sat atop a bluff at the mouth of the Chagres River. We had to have passage there, or we couldn't hope to reach Panama. Bradley led his men in a headlong charge, but the Spanish saw them coming and met them with such cannon fire that three dozen were killed in the first rush, and twice that many wounded. It settled down to a long day's exchange of gunfire. Bradley might have sent to me for aid, but that wasn't his way. I had told him to take the fort, and take it he would."

Uncle Patrick tied off the bandage. "There. That's done. Time to go, Davy lad."

"But the governor's story—"

"Will last all day and half the night, and Mrs. Cochran is waiting dinner on us."

Morgan waved his hand. "I'll cut it short, Patch. There was a double row of wooden stakes surrounding the fort. The Spanish were firing guns, throwing stones, whatever they could reach. One of them shot a man with an arrow. That made the lad angry. He tore the arrow from his own flesh, wrapped some gunpowder in a rag and tied it to the shaft of the arrow, lit it, and dropped it down his musket barrel. He fired it right back at the Spanish. It stuck in the roof of a building inside the fort and set that afire."

"A fine kind of warfare," grumbled my uncle.

"War is never pretty," Morgan told him flatly.

"Bradley realized what would happen and had some of his men set up a steady fire on the other side, drawing the Spanish away. Meanwhile he had a small group of soldiers throw grenades, just pots of gunpowder with fuses, against the palisades. They began to flame, too, and the Spanish could not be everywhere at once to put out the blazes. The fire burned for hours, finally opening a section of the double wall. That was when Bradley led the charge! A hundred brave lads rushed with him. The Spanish fired a cannon right into the ranks. The ball cut both of Bradley's legs off above the knees. Know what he did?"

"No, sir," I said, my mouth dry.

"He had a man tie off the stumps, then had himself propped against a tree, in plain view of the Spanish. He screamed his orders to his men as he lay there, propped and helpless and bleeding to death. He lived to see the fort taken, but 'tis one of my great regrets that he died of his wounds almost as soon as I arrived to congratulate him on his victory." With a sigh, Morgan pushed himself up from his chair. "And had he lived, his reward for the loss of his legs would have been eight hundred pieces of eight, for that was the rate back then."

"You did take Panama?" I asked.

With a chuckle, Morgan said, "So I did, so I did. And a hard fight I had of it, and a long yarn it is, so you'll not be hearing it this time, young Davy! Even Henry Morgan's not man enough to stand between Mollie Cochran and her schedules!" He reached for his cane and frowned. "I'm as weak as a kitten, Patch. To think that fifteen years ago I marched an army across to Panama, men dropping of fever all around me, and took the richest city in the New World! Now I'm little more than the king's lapdog, barking at the pirates in these parts."

"I've told you and told you," said my uncle in an exasperated tone, "If you would but be careful of your diet and your drinking, you—"

Morgan interrupted him: "Here you are, young David." He took a coin from his pocket and handed it to me.

I took the heavy silver coin from him. It was not perfectly round, but irregular. Stamped on it were a cross, two towers, and two lions. "A Spanish dollar," I said in delight.

"Pieces of eight," replied Morgan with a chuckle.

"Take that one. 'Tis part of the booty from Portobello, and perhaps it may bring you a bit of luck."

"Thank you, sir!"

Leaning heavily on his cane, Morgan walked slowly with us to the door. "Patch, what news have you heard of that villain Steele?" he asked.

"The devil a word have I heard of him, except from you," my uncle replied. "And you complain about him every time I see you. The man stays on your mind like a toothache!"

A map of the whole Gulf of Mexico and part of the Atlantic hung on the wall beside the door. Morgan pulled up short before it and exclaimed, "Devil take the man, Jack Steele is the worst villain ever to sail! Far worse than I ever was! He slaughters people for pleasure, that man. I'd gladly give both my legs if I could see that evil creature swinging from a yardarm!" He stabbed his finger out at the map, again and again. "Barbados! Steele killed thirty people there! Saint Kitts—burned a church, with women and children jammed inside! Curaçao—went in under a flag of truce and broke truce, killing three score or more! But never a

Spanish target does he pick. No, the Spanish love him!"

Uncle Patrick put a cautioning hand up. "Steady, Governor Morgan. You'll work yourself into a stroke!"

With a growl and a heavy sigh, Morgan shook his head. "If I could bring Jack Steele to justice, I'd be back in the king's good graces in no time, Patch. Then there'd be none of this nonsense about not allowing me to fill my seat on the council. But if I hope to catch him, I have to be quick about it. Not everyone in London is a friend to old Harry Morgan, and Lord knows I've enemies enough in Jamaica. And on top of that, I'm a dying man."

"You're a man careless of his health," my uncle returned. "Which is a far different thing indeed. Now Davy and I have to go. You take some rest, and you bear in mind what I've told you time and again."

"Aye, more rest, less rum, more vegetables, like some kind of elderly piratical rabbit. . . ."

We left him fuming there, and when we were far down the street, I turned back and saw the old buccaneer standing in his doorway, holding the door frame with both hands. He looked forlorn and angry and—I could not help thinking—lonely.

"Watch where you're going," Uncle Patrick warned me as I stumbled.

"I'm sorry." I felt the Spanish dollar in my pocket. "I've heard tales of Sir Henry. People say that he was bloodthirsty and vicious when he was a captain."

"So he was," shot back my uncle. "I'd be the last to deny it. Do you know the man captured priests, and when he stormed the fort at Portobello, he made them rush out to lean the ladders against the walls?"

I thought of Father Anthony, the priest who said Mass in a private home across the bay every Sunday. He was the one who heard our confessions, an old, white-haired man with a patient smile and a soft voice. "Surely that was a sin."

"Surely it was," Uncle Patrick agreed. "But to Morgan the greater sin would have been to leave the Spanish holding Portobello and to admit defeat. The man has a mind like a snake, with more twists and turns than you could well count. Faith, no wonder he was such a brilliant soldier. He saw his men as pawns, as puppets. No, they were more like his hands. And if Morgan wouldn't mind losing a leg or two to get what he's after, he'd have not a single thought about losing a finger—or a man."

"He seemed sad that Joseph Bradley died."

Uncle Patrick made an explosive little sound of disagreement. "Only that he did not live long enough to help Morgan take Panama. Sir Henry never thinks about yesterday. With him, the dead bury the dead. I'm sure the evening that he heard his dear friend Joseph Bradley had died, Morgan made an excellent supper and shed not a single tear nor lost a moment's sleep. I think the man would join forces with the devil himself if he thought it would advance England's cause one inch."

"Governor Morgan is a remarkable man," I said as we turned into an alley leading back to Thames Street.

"That he is, Davy lad," my uncle said in a strange voice. "That he is."

CHAPTER SIX

HMS Retribution

IT WAS BUT A FEW days later that Lieutenant Hunter met us at the door as we came home one evening. "Patch! There you are. I've news for you, my friend, and I hope you're in the mood to take it as it's offered."

"Depends on what it is, now, doesn't it?"

Lieutenant Hunter grabbed my uncle by the arm. "First, before anything else, you'd be ready to certify that I'm fit for sea duty again?"

"I might be," said my uncle. "But first let us in, or I'll certify only that you're keeping a thirsty man from his ale."

The three of us went into the small parlor, and

Uncle Patrick sent me to fetch two mugs of ale for him and the lieutenant. "You may have lemon-water yourself, if you've a thirst," he added.

I found Jessie, who for all her learning still treated me as though I were some kind of toad, and persuaded her to draw the ale and pour the lemonade. She put the mugs on a tray for me, with a grumble that I was keeping her from more important things, and I hurried back to the parlor with them. ". . . sure, I suppose you'd not hurt yourself at sea," my uncle was just saying. "You heal fast, and your scars are entirely healthy."

"Then—ah, thank you, Davy! Then to my news," said Lieutenant Hunter as he took a mug of ale from me, his red English face beaming. "There is a warship in harbor, and she wants a junior officer. What is more, Captain Brixton—for he is the commander of the frigate—tells me he wants a surgeon. He is willing to take me as a volunteer, and if you want a berth for a cruise or two, why, I'd stake my arm that he'd take you as well."

Uncle Patrick's eyes darted quickly toward me. "And what is Davy to do in the meantime?" he asked.

Mr. Hunter gave me the kindest smile. "Why, there are always boys aboard ship. Powder monkeys, midshipmen, captain's servants. Come to that, surgeons usually have loblolly boys, don't they?"

"They do," Uncle Patrick agreed readily. "But the term is elastic. It stretches to fit grown men strong enough to hold down a thrashing sailor while the surgeon saws off an arm or a leg."

"How was your voyage over?" Mr. Hunter asked me. "Were you seasick?"

"Not a bit of it!" I protested. "The Reverend Mr. Bonney was at the rail in every little blow of wind, but I kept my meals down the whole time!"

"Hunter," began my uncle in a warning tone.

"Perhaps you could try him on a short voyage," suggested the lieutenant. "And if he is not suitable, then he may tarry here ashore and wait for you. I make no doubt that you could ask Mr. Hardin or Mr. Athol to take over his education."

My uncle fairly snorted. "Hardin is a quack, and Athol is a drunkard," he said. "I'd as soon send the lad to the butcher's to learn surgery!" He drained the last of his ale. "Faith, this comes at an awkward time. What kind of skipper is this Captain Brixton?"

"A stern one, by all accounts," replied Mr. Hunter. "But most frigate-captains are. And he has a crew of the *right true British able-bodied sailors.*" Hunter said the last few words with peculiar emphasis and, I thought, a significant glance at my uncle.

"The ship?" asked Uncle Patrick with a resigned sigh.

"The HMS *Retribution*," answered Hunter at once. "A beauty. A twenty-eight-gun frigate, a hundred and ten feet in length and barely twenty-seven in the beam. Crew of one hundred and eighty-four, not counting the officers. The guns are twelve-pounders. A broadside weight of one hundred sixty-eight pounds! Why, a ship like that, properly manned, could take on anything short of a Spanish war galleon!"

"And I take it that Captain Brixton is looking for Jack Steele?"

"As is every honest captain in these waters," said Hunter. "It's a naval berth, not a pleasure cruise after all, and if we are called on to fight, why then we fight. Come on, Patch. Will you at least go see the ship with me tomorrow morning?"

My uncle sighed. "I suppose so. I would like to see whether my stitching I did holds you together while you do your job."

"May I come, too?" I asked.

Just for the instant, I'm pretty sure my uncle was on the verge of telling me no, but then up spoke Lieutenant Hunter again: "Oh, let him come along with us, Patch. It will do him no harm. I was a good year younger than he when I first set foot on a British warship."

"Aye," growled my uncle, "and see where it's got you!" But he left it at that, and all that evening I took special care to be obedient and handy. I did not intend to be left behind.

The next morning, as I have good reason to remember, was Thursday, August 18, 1687. It was a still, hot day, and though we rose early, the air lay breathless and steaming as the three of us made our way down to the docks. The *Retribution* was easy to pick out, a shark among minnows, a great warship lying at double anchor some little way out past the fishing and trading craft. Lieutenant Hunter hailed two enormous black boatmen loitering by the dock. "Ahoy, passage for two gentlemen and a lad to the *Retribution*?"

"Penny a head, Cap'n," the elder of the two called up.

"There and back?"

"Penny a head each way, Cap'n, an' cheap at th' price. We'll get you there dry, we will!"

"A deal, if you'll get us there lively!"

The big man chuckled. "Don't do nothin' but lively, Cap'n!" I had noticed before how the Jamaicans almost seemed to sing when they talked, with a kind of easy lilting music. The boatman had that kind of voice, in a deep bass tone.

We skimmed across the water, and the *Retribution* grew in my sight. Long and sleek, she was painted a stark black, save for her gunport lids, which were white. As we neared, a voice from the deck hailed us and demanded to know our business. "Lieutenant William Hunter, volunteer, come at the captain's orders," returned Mr. Hunter. "And a first-rate surgeon and his servant."

We were haled aboard. It was a puzzle to me, for we had to clamber up a sort of ladder built into the side of the ship. The steps were shallow, and the ropes were not much help. "Saints be with us," muttered my uncle. "I never liked this sort of housebreaker's clamber! You first, Davy."

"Me?"

"Wait for the next roll, young sir," chuckled one of the boatmen. "Or ye'll be swimmin'. I'll give ye a boost up, never mind."

When the side of the ship leaned away from us, the boatman gave me a hearty push. I leaped onto the ladder, seized the ropes in both hands, and scrambled up as well as I could, which was not very well at all. The last few steps were easier because the gunwales of the boat tapered inward. This was what they called the "tumblehome," and I well nigh gave truth to the name, for I came aboard almost falling. Lieutenant Hunter steadied me, then reached down a hand for my uncle. As soon as he was safely aboard, Hunter pitched a sixpenny piece into the boat. "Handsomely rowed! Stand by, and you shall have twice that again for taking us back!" he called cheerfully.

"Aye, aye, Cap'n!" sang back one of the boatmen. "Dawn down to dusk if need be!"

Hunter saluted the quarterdeck, and a tall, square-faced young man in the uniform of a lieutenant came forward to meet us. "Hunter," he said. "Glad to see you again."

"Twinings," replied Hunter civilly. "Permit me to name my friend and surgeon, Mr. Patrick Shea. This is his servant and nephew, David. Gentlemen, Mr. Harry Twinings, with whom I served when we were both mere midshipmen."

Twinings gave us both easy nods. "And now I glory in the title of first lieutenant of the *Retribution*. Captain Brixton is expecting you. I've sent a midshipman to tell him you're aboard."

And sure enough, a moment later, a breathless young man of sixteen came running back with the news, "Captain's compliments, and he will see you now."

We followed him back along the deck, past the mainmast, and through a narrow door. He led us down a short corridor, knocked at a door at the end of it, and opened it when we heard a gruff, "Come in!"

We stepped into the main cabin of the frigate. I thought it was pure glory. Windows let in bright daylight, windows that slanted outward. A portly, red-faced man sat at a desk, a quill in his hand. He glanced up at us. "Pray allow me to finish this letter. I have but to sign it." He took some time to read through what he had written, heaved a sigh, and put his name to it. "I hate writing to widows," he muttered. "So. You are William Hunter, are you?"

"Yes, sir," said Hunter, standing straight as a ramrod. "Late of the *Brilliant*, under Captain Carver."

"Ah," said Captain Brixton. "Too bad about Carver."

"Sir?" asked Hunter.

"You don't know?" asked Captain Brixton. "No, I suppose you would not have heard. The *Red Queen* fought it out with the *Brilliant* not three weeks ago in the Florida Strait. The *Brilliant* went down with all hands. A hundred and twenty men at a stroke! I had the news in Tortuga myself just a week ago, when we put in for water."

I thought Mr. Hunter's jaw looked as if he was clenching it. "I am sorry to hear it, sir. I had many friends aboard the *Brilliant*."

"Henry Carver was a good man," replied Captain Brixton. "Only shy of training his gunners. He should have known not to try to shoot it out with a ship the size of Steele's *Red Queen*. Curse the Dons for letting him steal the brute in the first place! However. Now, as I understand it, you are willing to come aboard as a volunteer?"

"Yes, sir."

Brixton nodded. "I could use you as third lieutenant. My own died of yellow fever. And this, I understand, is the surgeon?"

"Patrick Shea, sir," affirmed Mr. Hunter. "A physician in all but title, indeed, for he attended medical school at Trinity College in Dublin."

"So, so," said the captain. He held up the parchment he had just signed. "You would be most welcome, too, sir. This letter is to tell Mrs. Wright that she is a widow, her husband having died of the same fever as my third lieutenant. Mr. Wright, sir, was the ship's surgeon. You come as a volunteer?"

"For the time, sir, I may," returned my uncle. "May I have a look at the sick berth first?"

"Certainly," said the captain, gesturing to the

young midshipman. "Mr. Laughton, show Doctor Shea and this lad to the sick berth, then come back and stand by. My business with Lieutenant Hunter will occupy us for some little time yet."

We went forward and then belowdecks, to a long, narrow room lighted by a checkerboard of sun and shadow coming through an overhead hatch. Only one hammock was slung here, and from it a grizzled sailor raised his head. He looked at us and, with a gasp, let his head fall back again.

"What's your trouble, my man?" asked my uncle.

"Crushed toes, sir," said the sufferer weakly.

"Let's have a look." My uncle bent over the man's foot, which was swollen and purple. "And how did this happen?"

"Gun carriage, sir. I took an awkward step as it recoiled."

Uncle Patrick took off his coat and looked around. "Hang this somewhere. I'll warrant the late Mr. Wright's instruments are in this case." He pulled open a drawer or two as I found a peg on which to hang his coat. He must have discovered whatever he was looking for, because he bent over the sailor's foot and his arm gave a sudden twist.

The sailor's hands seized the sides of his hammock, and he cried out in surprise and pain. "Devil take you, you insane lubber! What are . . . ?"

Uncle Patrick held up something triangular. It was wet with blood and glistened as he turned it in his fingers. "Splinter of bone," he said. "I'll take a stitch or two here, and that should do for you, my man. Come here, Davy, and hold his ankle. He'll want to jerk that foot."

I grasped the man's bony ankle and held on hard while my uncle took one, two, three neat, quick stitches. "There!" he said cheerfully when he had finished. "We'll bandage that, and you'll be up again in a day or two and back to your duty in a week. You held still admirably well, my good fellow. Now, you were saying?"

"Thank you, sir," said the sailor in a weak voice.

"You're a man of fortitude, so you are," said my uncle comfortably as he wound the bandage on. "As inflamed as that great toe of yours was, that must have hurt like the very devil. I'll ask the captain about an extra tot of rum for you. What's your name?"

"Saunders, sir, foretopman."

"Well done, Saunders. You may call me Patch, if you like. I'm to be surgeon here, apparently."

Saunders lay breathing hard while my uncle toured the sick berth. "Good chest of medicines, very little to buy. Instruments are first-rate. I wonder, now, whether they are the ship's or Wright's? I think I'll ask if a wind-sail could be rigged. I like a well-aired sick berth best."

"Are you going to take the position, then?" I asked.

"If the captain likes, I'll take it on trial, for the first voyage," my uncle said. "Of course, there is the question of what to do with the likes of you, for I'd not wish those two blockheads Hardin and Athol on you for a million pounds."

"Are they the surgeons that Mr. Hunter mentioned?"

"If your definition of a surgeon is any blessed fool who can pick up a scalpel without needing stitches himself, then aye!"

"Let me stay aboard with you, then," I begged. "I'll be your loblolly boy, whatever that is!"

Uncle Patrick laughed as he led me to a companionway and up onto the deck. As we emerged into the sunshine, he muttered, "Faith, I've left my coat behind. Nip down for it, Davy, like a good lad."

I hurried back to the sick berth. Saunders again looked up as I came in. "Is it true? Is that man to be our surgeon?"

"He says so," I told the sailor.

"'Tis well," Saunders pronounced. "My foot's been an agony to me for days, and now it's more easy like. I was feared Cap'n would send me ashore, and the landlubber doctors would have it off. 'Patch' he says to call him, hey? 'Tis a good name for a surgeon, to be sure, Patch." He lay back with a kind of chuckle.

"Thank you, Davy," said my uncle when I came back on deck and handed him his jacket. "All right, here's the way of it: I shall ask Captain Brixton if you may accompany me as servant on the first voyage he proposes, which I understand will be an easy one of three or four months. After that time, though, if I decide to stay aboard, you shall go ashore with such provision as I can make for you— and no arguments!"

"No, sir. Thank you, sir," I said, knowing in truth

that this was not the time to argue with him for a longer stay on the ship.

I had three or four months to do that.

"Stay out of trouble for five minutes, then," he told me, and he went back toward the captain's cabin.

It was longer than five minutes, but the time flew. I spent it looking up at the masts, where three parties of sailors were busy as spiders rerigging lines through blocks and making all fast with quick knots. One of them leaped out from a yard's end, making the heart of me rise to my throat, but quick as a monkey he seized a line and slid down it, coming to the deck with a light thump. He gave me a curious look, but hurried away, and came back again with a coil of twine carried over his shoulder. He swung out and went up the starboard shrouds, nimble as a cat climbing a tree. He reached the foretop and scrambled up the futtock shrouds, hanging backwards over the deck for a moment before he was safe and sound in the top itself.

"Very well," came the captain's voice behind me. "You shall have volunteer's pay and a share of any prize money we should chance to come by. And your nephew can berth with the squeakers."

"Thank you, sir," said my uncle, emerging onto deck just behind Captain Brixton. "And pray do not forget about the rum for Saunders. 'Tis medicinal in this case."

"Don't make a practice of prescribing it, sir, or every man Jack aboard will report ill. But Saunders is a good hand, and I'll send down my own servant with a double tot for him. Report aboard with your dunnage before noon tomorrow, Mr. Shea," the captain ordered. "For I mean to sail with the evening tide."

"Come, Davy," my uncle ordered. "Mr. Hunter is going to remain aboard for some time, so the two of us will take the boat back."

If climbing up into the ship had been a strain, going down into the boat was even worse. One of the good-humored boatmen reached up and guided my steps down with his hands, but even so, more than once I came close to slipping. At last, though, I sat on the thwart of the boat and watched my uncle come down. If I had been as ungainly a sight as he, no wonder our two boatmen were smiling so broadly.

At the dock, Uncle Patrick gave them another sixpence, muttering, "Blast William Hunter! 'Tis easy to double the fee when he's not the one coming back!" The day was torrid as we walked toward the inn. My uncle was his usual taciturn self, but I was fair bursting with questions. "Sir," I got up the nerve to say, "what did the captain mean, 'squeakers'?"

"Navy talk, nephew," answered Uncle Patrick. "Midshipmen, the young'uns. He hasn't many this voyage, three or four, I think, and you'll sleep in their berth, in a hammock. You'll have all of sixty inches to yourself, so it's likely you'll feel crowded."

"And what does a loblolly boy do, sir?"

"Whatever he's told." After a moment or two, my uncle added, "A loblolly boy is a surgeon's general servant for running and carrying. I may let you help me compound some medicines, if you're careful enough not to poison our patients. You'll announce sick call every day and see that the men take whatever doses I call for. And sometimes you may have to help me if I must operate."

As we neared the inn, he began to whistle some jaunty tune, a sailor's hornpipe, I thought. "And is it happy you are to be at sea again?" I asked.

He chuckled. "Faith, at least I'm happy to see you happy." He paused at the inn door and clapped a hand on my shoulder. "Only understand this, Davy Shea: You are not to expect every day aboard a king's ship to be a holiday. No, it's bad food, work, and blessed hard work at that, with long hours, and a fair chance of drowning or of being blown to kingdom come, all thrown into the bargain. Not to mention bloody decks that don't stay in the same place from one second to the next."

"Sir," I said, "I'm looking forward to it."

And Lord help me, on that eighteenth of August, so I was, having no notion at all of the terrible great change that just three short weeks could make.

The Mutiny

IT TOOK BUT A FEW days at sea to teach me well that my uncle was not exaggerating. It seemed that the term "loblolly boy" was indeed elastic, for it stretched far enough to make me have to run for this, carry that, and fetch the other, at all hours of the day or night.

We had not well sunk the land behind us when I began to learn about my shipmates. The midshipmen's berth held five of us. Mr. Adams, a skinny young man with a sad face, was the oldest, at twenty-four. He was the captain of the berth, he told me shortly, and it was he who assigned me to a small little kind of booth, with hooks for my hammock and very little else. It was not closed off, but open to the main compartment of the berth, so the snores of the others rasped loud in my ears as I tried to sleep.

Mr. Adams told me in a gloomy voice that he had all but given up being made lieutenant. "I don't have the head for the mathematics," he complained. "I can't work out our position on a chart to within a hundred miles, and no matter how I try, I cannot grasp the mathematics of leeway and sun sights and such." But he was kind enough in his way, and he introduced me to the others.

After Mr. Adams came Mr. Laughton, a heavy boy of sixteen. He had been born in the Virginia colony and had a strange way of speaking, to my ear. The first night I was aboard the *Retribution*, I swung into my hammock, and to my shock it fell with me splat to the deck. Mr. Laughton, who kept his hair cut short, had to hold his sides to keep from splitting with laughter. I found that the loop of rope holding the foot of my hammock had been cut almost through, and it took no great brains to realize that Laughton was the culprit. He loved to play tricks, and more than once I had to hold in my temper to keep from giving him a bloody nose.

The other two midshipmen were Mr. Kimball, who was a sturdy boy of thirteen, and Mr. Raymond, who was just my own age. Of them all, they treated me the kindest, for they began to teach me the ropes straight away.

It was on the second morning out that Mr. Raymond, a lively boy who was nearly half a head shorter than I, winked at me and said, "Come on, then. Time to see what's what." He swung out over the net holding the rolled-up hammocks of the crew, grabbed the shrouds, and started up toward the maintop. "Come on!" he called again.

Taking my courage in my hands, I gingerly swung my leg over the hammock net and grabbed the ropes. "Not those," said Mr. Kimball, just behind me. "Hold on to the up-and-down ones, the shrouds. You step on the going-across ones. Those we call the ratlines."

It was a hard climb for me, but Mr. Kimball was just below, calling up encouragement. "You'll soon be used to it," he said. "Step, step, step. Hold on tight, and don't look down!"

I reached the futtock shrouds and stopped,

puzzled as to how to proceed. The futtock shrouds were made fast to the main shrouds, but they led up and backwards to the edge of the top, a wooden platform about six feet wide. I could worm through them and come up through the hole in the top where the shrouds went around the mast, but nobody else did. Bobby Raymond stuck his grinning face out over the edge of the top and said, "Clap on to the futtock shrouds and wait for the roll. Then I'll give you a hand up!"

I clutched the ropes desperately as the ship rolled toward me, making me hang almost completely upside down like a sloth. Then the ship rolled the other way, and Raymond reached a hand down. "Up and over!"

With him pulling and me struggling, I somehow or other came over the top, and a moment later, Mr. Kimball swung up, all smiles. "Not bad for a first try," he said. He and Mr. Raymond stood up. "Good view from here."

With one hand on the mast, I forced my knees to straighten themselves. Quickly I grabbed for a rope. "Not that!" yelled Mr. Kimball. "Here, hold this, if you want. A stay, not a working line."

For the first time I dared look down. We were eighty-some feet above the deck, and with every roll of the ship the mast took us maybe 150 feet from left to front to right to back to left again. But it was a grand sight to look down and see the white water curving from the bow, and the wake stretching out behind us on a blue, blue sea.

"Next lesson," said Mr. Raymond, "is how to get down." And he leaped into space, making me yelp. But he seized hold of a stay and slid down it, looking up, his grinning face growing smaller by the moment.

"Or farther up," added Mr. Kimball, and he scuttled up, up the stays to the very masthead, another thirty feet above my head.

I decided it would be more prudent for me to go down the way I had come up. Getting back to the shrouds was fairly easy. Climbing back down, with no one to guide my feet, was something else. Men swarmed up past me when I was barely started down, roughly telling me to move aside. I had nowhere to go, however, and they had to shove past any way. They began to work the sails, the ship took on more speed and gave a lurch, and with a cry of alarm I lost my grip and fell back and down. By luck, the crooks of my legs caught on a ratline, and I dangled there upside down.

In a flash, Kimball was with me, laughing. "Don't be frightened," he said.

My eyes felt as if they were bugging from my head, but I gave him a patient look. "Sure, I'm only enjoying the fresh air. I find that a change of position eases me now and then."

Raymond joined us, and between the two of them, they got me straightened out and headed down, but they had to climb up to help with the sail changing, Raymond on the mainmast, Kimball on the mizzen. My uncle met me as I stepped around the shrouds and leaped back onto the deck. "Since you have time for skylarking," he said sternly, "I shall have to find you a few tasks to do."

"Yes, sir."

He found a good many, enough to keep me busy for hours on end. Still, I gradually learned to climb the shrouds without feeling as if I was about to plunge to the deck. After a few days, I could even stand at ease in the tops, though to be sure I lacked the nerve to swing on a line's end from mast to mast as the others did.

The naval day began at noon, with Captain Brixton and his mates taking a sight on the sun with their cross-staves. Our lives were lived to the chime of bells marking off the half hours. At four bells in the afternoon watch—or what I used to call two o'clock—I stood on deck beating a drum and feeling foolish as I sang out a rhyme:

> "All ye sailors, hear o hear!
> Ye may see your doctor dear!
> If ye have hurt or sickness' smart,
> Come and he will ease your heart!"

"Faith, Uncle, but this is silly stuff," I'd complained the first time he'd run the words by me.

He gave a short creaking laugh of agreement. "Aye, silly it may be, and childish to boot, but from time out of mind, the crew of a man o' war expects their sick call to be announced in just such a fashion, and to do anything else would be to make them uneasy in their minds."

Rarely did we have much to do, for it was by and

large a healthy crew. We treated some sprains and some strains, some rope burns and some cases of constipation, but nothing serious, neither disease nor injury. As soon as sick call ended, my uncle sat me down to continue our lessons. Thinking that if I did well he would let me stay on after our first voyage, I studied with a will.

Lieutenant Hunter, being the third mate aboard the frigate, was similarly busy. Yet he found time to talk with us. Indeed, whenever he was not on duty or wanted on deck, Mr. Hunter was always talking to Uncle Patrick about this, that, and the other. Once he made some angry remark about Jack Steele, and my uncle shook his head. "You have bitterness in your heart, Hunter," he observed. "And that's a poison for which there is no antidote."

"I have reason enough to be bitter!" flashed out the young lieutenant, his expression surprisingly angry. "My father and my mother—the villain killed both of them."

I must have squeaked out, being startled. Uncle Patrick darted a frowning glance my way. "Hush, and don't think of it," he said to Hunter.

Hunter looked at me with a twisted smile. "Oh, I

don't mind if Davy knows. We're orphans together, after all. Davy, my father held a grant of land in the Virginia colony, and seven years ago, he decided to sail from England to inspect it. My mother had always longed to travel, and so the two of them crossed the sea on a merchant vessel that my father owned, the *Virginia Grace*. I was still a midshipman then, and halfway around the world, so I heard all this secondhand later on. Off Bermuda, Jack Steele took the *Virginia Grace* and all aboard. Some few he ransomed back again. After he had looted the ship thoroughly, he forced most of the others into her, sailed some distance off, and deliberately fired into the hulk until it sank. Sixty people went down with her, along with them my father and my mother."

"But if your father owned the ship, surely he could have paid a ransom," I said.

"Aye, he had the money to do so, but he fought Steele face-to-face and defied the man with curses. For his pains, my father got a scornful laugh from Steele, and death for him and my mother. Father never was a prudent man. Anyway, one lone sailor survived by floating on a grating that separated from the sinking *Virginia Grace*, and he was picked up a few days later. He told me the tale himself. From the moment I heard the story, I hated Steele. One day I shall see him hanging, and then I may rest easy."

From the look on Mr. Hunter's face, I would not have been in Jack Steele's boots for any money.

We were bound for the Massachusetts Bay, and Captain Brixton drove us hard enough. As we came into colder waters, the sea grew rough, and we began to see more injuries in the sick berth. My uncle's expression became grim as Brixton insisted that any man able to walk was able to work.

As my uncle had warned, the food was very bad. It had not been properly stored, and the salt pork and beef in the barrels had probably crossed the ocean five or six times. Some of it was plainly rotten, and the ship's biscuit crawled with weevils and maggots. I soon learned to follow the midshipmen's example and tap the hard bread on the table for half a minute, shaking out most of the creatures before I dared to eat.

We lost a topsail off the Carolinas in a hard gale, and that seemed to anger the captain beyond all reason. With the rain and the spray whipping into his face, he shouted, "Until you learn to be seamen, you'll have no more rum aboard this ship!" And the rum ration, which the sailors held to be one of their chief rewards, was stopped from that moment on, to great grumbling.

We made poor northing, for storm after storm hit us, and we frequently found ourselves driven to the south, running under just enough sail to keep from turning sideways to the wind and broaching to—rolling over and sinking. After a particularly heavy blow, a Monday morning came when, for the first time, the captain dealt out punishment.

A foretopman, Abel Tate, had protested when ordered to go aloft during the storm to let a reef out of a sail—indeed, the very sail that could not hold and that blew clean out of its bolt-ropes and away on the gale. Mr. Hunter had mildly scolded him, and Tate had at last done his duty, but to Tate's bad fortune, Captain Brixton had heard something of the argument.

That Monday, therefore, the captain had Tate brought before him. The captain stood on the quarterdeck looking down with a displeased glint in his eye, and the short, wiry Tate waited below him in the waist of the ship, his head bowed and his attitude meek.

When the captain spoke, his voice rolled like the crack of doom: "Abel Tate, speaking back to an officer is a serious offense. It is insubordination, and I will not tolerate insubordination on my ship! Punishment is twelve lashes. Bosun, carry out the punishment."

Lieutenant Hunter seemed surprised at that, and he spoke up: "Sir, with submission, I do not think that Tate offered any ill will. He only thought it an awkward time to make more sail, and he said as much. I was not angry with him."

Captain Brixton's face flamed like a furnace full of red-hot coals. "Hold your tongue, sir! I decide what is justice aboard this ship! Bosun, seize that man to a grating and carry out the sentence!"

"Sir," said Hunter desperately, "surely twelve lashes is harsh for what the man did!"

"Make that four-and-twenty lashes, Bosun! And if Mr. Hunter speaks again, I shall add another dozen for each one of his words!"

By now looking miserable and frightened, poor

Tate shook his head. I thought he was silently pleading to Mr. Hunter, asking him to keep still. The bosun's men stripped the shirt from Tate's back and tied his hands to a grating tilted against a bulkhead. Then the bosun, a strongly built man, let the cat out of the bag, taking out his cat-o'-nine-tails, a wicked whip. He took two steps and a kind of skip and brought the lash down against poor Tate's naked back with a crack like a pistol shot. Tate threw his head back, his teeth clenched in agony, and spittle drooled from his mouth, but he did not cry out. I had to look away, but I counted the lashes: a dozen. Fifteen. Twenty. And, at last, twenty-four. "Cut him down," said the captain. "Take him to sick berth."

Hunter's face was clouded with dark anger. We got poor Tate, wholly unconscious, to the sick berth. "Don't watch this, Davy," muttered Uncle Patrick. "'Tis ghastly to see." He blocked my view as he dressed Tate's blood-streaked back. Hunter came in just as he had finished and as our patient was coming around. "Tate, my man, I'm sorry for you," said Lieutenant Hunter.

"You tried, sir," answered the unfortunate sailor.

"The captain's a hard-horse officer, and no mistake. He's denied shore leave before, but this voyage he's dealing out lashes something cruel. But I don't mean to complain, sir."

"Something should be done about such men," Hunter asserted. "And by heaven, one of these days something will be!"

That was the night of September 8. It was just three weeks since we had come aboard. We should have been far to the north, but we had lost so much headway that we were only a few hundred miles north of Hispaniola. The storms had finally left us, and we seemed to be running pretty easily under plain sail.

I turned in, dead tired, and soon was asleep, for I truly believe there is no more restful bed in the world than a hammock aboard a smooth-sailing ship.

It must have been well past midnight that something woke me up. I came from sleep with a start, and then I heard again the sound that had broken through to me: the clang and clash of cutlasses! Had pirates boarded us? I swung from my hammock, dressed just in my breeches, and pulled on a shirt. No one else was in the midshipmen's berth, and I could find no lantern. Barefoot, moving by touch alone, I hurried to the companionway to climb onto the deck and learn what was afoot. The whole time, the sounds from above became louder and more alarming, shouts and curses, the explosion of a pistol. I came up through the fore hatchway, onto a deck crowded with jostling, shouting men.

I turned toward the quarterdeck. In the flaring light of the stern lanterns, the captain stood at the rail, a pistol in his hands. "Down, you mutinous dogs!" he roared.

"We'll have no more of your tyranny, Captain Brixton!" shouted a man—to my shock, it was Lieutenant Hunter! And at his back, fifteen or twenty of the sailors brandished cutlasses and shouted agreement.

"I'll see the color of his blood!" yelled one, clambering to the gangway and running toward the captain, flourishing his sword. It was Abel Tate, the back of his shirt streaked with dark blood.

Very deliberately, the captain lowered his pistol,

aimed, and when Tate was only steps away, he fired! Tate screamed, jerked, and his cutlass flew from his hand, spinning overboard. He toppled from the gangway to the deck, and his mates caught the poor fellow. "You've killed him!" some shouted.

The captain had drawn another pistol, and he aimed it at Mr. Hunter. "And so I shall you, if you do not this instant lay down your weapon! Marines! Fire into them at my command!"

I heard the clatter as half a dozen marines stepped forward from behind the captain, bringing their muskets up.

"Lay down your swords, lads!" commanded Lieutenant Hunter. "We stand no chance here!"

With the clash of metal, the sailors threw their swords to the deck. The captain nodded, his face a mask of cold fury. "I shall see you all hanged for this mutiny," he announced. "You mutineers, take that body below and sew it into a hammock. Marines, when they have done that, clap them in irons! Have the surgeon, this rascal's friend, treat the wounded. And when he's finished, throw him in irons, too! I shall have no rebellious Irishmen stirring up mutiny aboard my ship!"

I sank back down into the hold, unnoticed. But my heart was beating like a hammer, and my head was spinning. Mutiny? The worst crime a sailor could commit! And Mr. Hunter their leader? Worse, my uncle caught in the net as well?

What would become of him?

And, for that matter, what would become of me?

CHAPTER EIGHT

Death by Hanging

"COME IN!" The captain's voice, coming from within the main cabin, sounded harsh and rough.

The marine who had escorted me back opened the door and said, "Surgeon's boy asking to see you, sir."

Milky dawn light was beginning to pour through the stern windows of the *Retribution*. Captain Brixton sat at his desk, glowering at me. "Come in, then, and be quick about it. Stand to attention, there! Now what did you want of me, boy?"

"Sir," I said hesitantly, "I came to ask what is to be done with my uncle."

"Ha!" roared the captain, murder in his eye. "Mr.

Shea is to be tried with the other mutinous hounds, just as you might expect. I've given orders to take the ship back to Jamaica. There, a naval court will deal with these devils, giving them the only justice a mutineer deserves."

His face was so red and ferocious that he seemed to be another person entirely, not the captain who had agreed to have us come aboard. It took me some moments to work up the nerve to speak to him, so angry he seemed. In a meek voice, I began softly, "But, sir, my uncle never—"

"If you mind your behavior, boy, I will not throw you into irons with the others," the captain said as if I'd never spoken. "Though an Irish rebel like yourself probably deserves to be chained right next to your treacherous kin! So hear me well: Keep from underfoot, and stay out of my path, or you will quickly find the navy knows full well how to deal with impertinence!"

"But, sir—"

The captain brought the palm of his hand crashing down on the desk before him, making me jump. "That is all! Out of my sight, boy!"

Defeated, afraid, and with my head all in a whirl,

I retreated. On deck, I saw a dreadful sight. Two sailors were lugging a sort of man-sized parcel, a body sewn up into a hammock. Abel Tate's body, I realized, and watched in horror as they swung it back and forth one, two, three times, and then heaved it over the rail and into the ocean as if it were garbage. Never a prayer, never a kind word did they spare for their shipmate.

Down in the midshipmen's berth, I noticed that our disappointed and unmathematical elder midshipman, Mr. Adams, was missing, and all his things were gone. A very pale and subdued Mr. Laughton stood there sweating like a fat rainstorm. "Say a prayer for me, Shea, for I am now senior member of our company."

"Faith, and why?"

"Did ye not know? Mr. Adams was with the mutineers!"

"Where are they?" I asked.

"In the hold," said Mr. Laughton, all traces of humor gone from his face. "Chained like dogs, they are."

"May I see my uncle?" I asked without much hope.

Mr. Laughton's pasty complexion turned almost green with fear. "No! No chance of that! In fact, you'd best not leave the berth at all! If you try to see the prisoners, who'll be blamed for it? Me, that's who! And if you so much as put a foot on deck without my permission, I'll—I'll have you tied to a grating and the flesh whipped off your back!"

"You will?" I asked, showing a flash of temper.

He gave me a sick look. "Oh, Lord, probably not. Look, Davy, just stay below. The whole crew heard the captain yelling at you—it's not fair, not by a long shot, but do it just the same or we're all in chains!"

With a fair following wind for a change, we took just a week to sail back to Jamaica, but during all that time never could I find a way to sneak into the hold and speak to Uncle Patrick, for guards were everywhere. I crept about very meekly, hardly daring to breathe in the presence of the officers, and the heart within me sank like a stone. Bobby Raymond felt sorry for me, or so he said, but he took great relish in foretelling my uncle's fate: "They'll run him up to the yardarm, sure. Have you ever seen a man hanged, Shea?"

When I shook my head, he sighed. "I did, once. The fool struck an officer, or so they told me. They led him up onto the deck blubbering, with his hands tied behind him. He was crying and begging for his life the whole time the master was reading out the sentence. And then they put a black bag over his head and a hemp noose around his neck, and six men grabbed hold of the line and at a trot they hauled him up to the yardarm, kicking and choking." Raymond shivered. "It's an ugly way to die, death by hanging."

I imagined the pressure of a rope on my own neck, and I swallowed hard. "Maybe they won't hang," I said.

"No fear of that," he returned. "For the punishment for mutiny is prescribed. They need only to gather enough senior officers for the court-martial, and then they'll all dance the hangman's jig, with their feet kicking in the air. I'm sorry for your uncle. He was a good man."

"Was. Faith, people are thinking already of my uncle as dead and gone," I muttered bitterly. "Yet what has he done? He wasn't even on deck during the fight, and never a word of encouragement have

I ever heard him speak to any mutineer. For the life of me, I cannot see how he can be guilty of anything more than being William Hunter's friend!"

Raymond nodded sharply. "Just so. And that will be enough for any court. Your uncle wouldn't have even been on board if it weren't for Mr. Hunter!"

When we anchored in Port Royal Bay, I went ashore with one of the first boats and made my way to The King's Mercy. Moll Cochran met me at the door with a "Bless my soul, what's this? Back already from the Massachusetts plantations?"

"Oh, Mrs. Cochran," I said, and then I'm afraid I burst into tears. It took a long time, but finally I choked out the whole dismal story. She hugged me and patted my hair and said, "There, there, lamb," but she could offer no real comfort.

The very next day, she took me to Fort Charles, where the trial was to be held. "Look out," she muttered as we wove our way through the crowd. "Step aside there . . . lively, now, lively . . . aye, you're a right gentleman, you are. . . ." Somehow she jostled us through the throng until we emerged in an arched opening looking out into the main courtyard. In the sun, five captains sat at a long table before us, none of them looking cheerful. Past the table, I saw my uncle standing beside William Hunter, and around the two of them the rest of the mutineers, Mr. Adams and all, a total of twenty-three men. None of them looked as if he expected mercy, or even justice, from that hard-faced set of captains. And they all wore chains on their wrists and ankles. It pained me to see my uncle treated so, like a common criminal.

I remember almost nothing of the trial. It was short, less than two hours long, and all the men were tried together, with scarcely any chance to say one word in their own defense. Captain Brixton, though, spoke at length, telling of a growing dissatisfaction and an increasing lack of obedience on the ship. The captains plainly took his testimony to heart, for, shaking their heads and murmuring amongst themselves, they glowered most unforgivingly at the prisoners. And at last the trial ended just as Mr. Raymond had predicted, with twenty-three dread sentences of "to be hanged by the neck until dead."

"Oh, Mrs. Cochran," I said, "what am I to do?"

"We'll think of something," she assured me, putting her arm around my shoulder.

The first thing I could think of was to go to Government House, to beg an audience with acting Governor Molesworth. I thought if I showed him how it was, and persuaded him that my uncle was entirely innocent of the mutiny, he might be able to do something. But Government House was in Spanish Town, fourteen or fifteen miles away inland, and to get there I had to hire a horse. Using some of the money that my uncle had left at the inn, I did so, and rode a gray ambling mare that looked as if she only wanted to find a place to lie down and die. With her slow pace, it took me hours to find the place, and once there I was turned away sharply without so much as the breath of a chance of speaking to the governor.

My next thought was that Sir Henry Morgan might have a word of comfort or a plan of help. 'Twas late evening by the time I got back to Port Royal and to his house, but though he saw me willingly enough, he offered me no hope.

"But is there nothing you can do, sir?" I asked as he shook his head heavily at the end of my story.

"Right now a word from me is likely to get him hanged sooner than later." He sighed. "Understand this, Davy Shea," he said gravely. "The Crown is not used to showing mercy to mutineers and pirates, and certainly not to misbegotten Irishmen. Your surest hope is to live with the Cochrans as best you can, for to your unhappy uncle you must say farewell. Nothing can save him now, no, not if the Angel Gabriel himself came to earth to plead for him. Sentence has been pronounced, and he is as good as dead."

Back at The King's Mercy, Jessie herself met me with more terrible news: "The sentence is to be carried out in two days' time," she said breathlessly. "They're to be hanged at Fort Charles, in the same courtyard where the trial was held. They say the soldiers are building the gallows now."

I groaned. Fort Charles was one of the five or six forts protecting the harbor, a great redbrick structure with thick walls crowned with battlements and bristling with great cannons. From its walls there could be no hope of escape, once the prisoners were inside. And now Jessie was telling me that my uncle would die on Friday.

"'Tis a plan I must think of," I said. "I have to see my uncle. At the least, I have to ask his blessing and say a farewell to him. 'Twould break my heart not to do that, and he the only family I have in the world."

"How will you get in to see him?" demanded Jessie. "He'll be under guard the whole time until—"

She did not finish but just stood there with her fist held up to her mouth. I sat in the little parlor turning ways and ways over in my mind, and Moll Cochran, bless her, came to sit with me. "'Tis no use at all," I said as night gathered outside. "I'm not devious enough for this."

"Aye," said Moll. "You'd need a corkscrew of a mind to find a way out of this trouble, a mind like your uncle has."

"If I could only think of a way to see him, now," I said in despair.

Moll Cochran's face hardened. "No! Put that clean from your mind. It's the very worst thing you could try. To you, Patrick Shea must be dead from this hour on, for there's no way you can be of help to him."

"At least I have to say good-bye to him," I protested. "Think of how sad it will be for him to go to his death with no word of farewell."

For a moment, Moll said nothing. Then she cleared her throat. "I've had a message from him that he does not want to see you," she said deliberately. "And that's an end to it. You are not to leave this house, Davy Shea! I'll keep a sharp eye on you until—until after Friday."

She left me, but Jessie peeked in not a moment later. "Don't listen to my mother," she said softly, though her freckled face was still set in a frown of disapproval. I supposed she was trying to be sympathetic, only she didn't know how. "If I were you, I'd go see him. Surely they'll let his only living relation in to say good-bye." Though I'm sure the words were kindly meant, she still sounded as if she were scolding me.

I spread my hands helplessly. "But where is he being kept? I don't even know that. If he's imprisoned in the fort—"

"He is not," said Jessie quickly. "I've heard the soldiers talking about it all day. All twenty-three of the prisoners are locked up in the Tabby House.

That's an old jail at the south end of Lime Street, on the corner of Cannon Street, not far from the fort."

"Do you think I can get in, then?"

She frowned at me. "How do I know? But if my uncle were in prison there, I'd find a way to get in! I might have to cry, and I might have to lie, but I'd find some way!"

I took a deep breath. "As to lying, why, though it is not a skill I've practiced much, except when I've had to, I could do it well enough. And if tears will get me in to see my uncle, I'll do my best to shed them by the bucket."

"It's not enough to talk about it, Davy Shea!"

"All right," I said. "I'll try."

"See that you do!"

Though, Lord help me, I had scarcely any hope that either my uncle or I would be the better for my trying.

It was even harder than I had expected. I rose well before sunup the next morning, washed myself as quickly and as quietly as I could, and put on my good suit, the one I had worn to see my mother buried. My uncle had had it cleaned and brushed and pressed, and if not as fine as new, it still made me at least presentable. I splashed water on my red hair and combed it as well as I could by the feeble light of one tallow candle and the dim help of a cracked little mirror tacked up on the wall of my bedroom.

I went down the stairs on tiptoe, my shoes in my hand, for I was afraid of waking Mrs. Cochran. And, bad luck of all bad luck, at the foot of the stairs stood Jessie Cochran, her hands on her hips.

I froze. "I suppose you're going to tell your mother," I whispered.

"No, you great mooncalf," she shot back, though she was whispering as well. "I'm here to help you. You can't lock the door behind you, and if it isn't locked, Mother'll know you've gone. She'll send someone looking for you, sure, if you don't get quickly away."

But I had thought already of the door, and to show her that I wasn't as stupid as she assumed, I said very coldly, "I was going to climb out a window."

"And tear that suit to pieces? Or sprain your fool ankle? And then what would you do with the only decent doctor in Port Royal about to hang? Just like a boy! Come on, hurry. And put your shoes on your feet, for heaven's sake. You look like a fool."

She opened the door, softly, and I stepped out and hurriedly drew my shoes on over my stockinged feet. "But why are you helping me?" I asked beneath the yellow lantern. "You don't even like me!"

"That's true enough," she said gruffly. "You're a pretty stupid boy, taken all in all, and more trouble than you're worth. But family is more important than liking, I reckon. Family helps family, always, and you're the only family Doctor Patch has! Beside, you taught me reading and you didn't have to. So be off with you, and good luck. You great mooncalf."

She shut the door behind me, and then came the click of the lock. I hurried down the dark street, all the way to the end, where an alley leading to Lime Street cut off to the left. Lime Street ran southward, almost straight to the red fort where my uncle was fated to die. It was a breezy morning, with clouds overhead, now and then showing through breaks a sprinkle of stars. I had cut it close, for the east was already growing red with the rising sun.

All the way I hurried, and all the way I kept running over in my mind what words I would say to my uncle, if I could even talk my way in to see him. Or was there possibly another way I might help with more than words? Might I smuggle in a pistol, perhaps, or a knife? No, for I'd be sure to be searched, and then it would be the gallows for me. What on earth could I offer Uncle Patrick except a tearful farewell that he probably did not wish, anyway? I did not know.

The red sun was peeking up as I got to the end of Lime Street. The Tabby House was a square old building in great disrepair. Its red tile roof was crumbling, and the splotchy gray walls were pockmarked and cracked. It was called the Tabby House, I guessed, because it was made of tabby, a peculiar kind of cement that used heaps and heaps of oyster shells. The windows all were shuttered and barred, and two guards, both holding muskets, stood at the only door I could see.

And now that I was there, I could hardly think of how to begin. Would these soldiers pay a boy of twelve any attention at all? It seemed the dream of a dream to hope so. But soldiers would have a commander, and a commander might listen to the plea of a relative.

I loitered about for half an hour, with the sun coming up and then vanishing behind a rack of gray cloud, hurried along by the wind. We were in for another blow, perhaps a hurricane, and every moment the gusts grew stronger, rattling the leaves of the gumbo-limbo trees, raising a cloud of dust in the streets. I wished my courage would rise like this wild wind. It flung a handful of dirt in the faces of the guards, and both of them coughed and bent to wipe their eyes. I thought my moment had at last come, and I squared my shoulders.

With fear and determination fighting within me, I took five steps toward the gray house.

And before I could take the sixth, the whole side wall exploded in a wave of heat and a shattering roar. The blast threw me to my knees, my ears ringing. Both the guards fell sprawling, and both lost their muskets in the fall. Clouds of smoke and dust boiled out.

And then from the gray, swirling cloud stepped a dead man.

CHAPTER NINE

The Escape

SOMEHOW I HAD NOT been hit by any of the melon-sized chunks of tabby blasted away when the whole side of the jail had blown up. Still, I felt as if a giant's fist had hit me hard in the stomach, taking the breath from my lungs and making the day go dark.

The morning air was thick with blown dust, whipping away on the wind, and it stank with the sharp burning reek of gunpowder. I sat leaning back in the street, my legs stretched out before me, my hands thrown back to support my weight, and my head spinning. As if in a dream in which everything moved slowly, I watched one of the soldiers crawl forward on hands and knees to clutch his fallen musket.

And then Abel Tate, or his ghost, took three long steps out of his cloud of dust and gently touched the point of his cutlass to the soldier's throat. The boy froze, the musket inches off the ground. In a good-humored voice, Tate said, "Lad, they don't pay you enough for that."

The soldier swallowed so hard that I saw his Adam's apple bob up and down. He rose to his knees and, with a sudden jerk of his arms, he tossed the musket as far down the street as he could. "You're right about that, mate."

"Good lad. Now get out of the way. You're blocking the street," Tate said, and he whistled shrilly through his teeth.

By that time I was trying to get to my feet, though I swear the ground beneath me was heaving like a stormy sea. Or maybe it was all in my buzzing head, where the echoes of the explosion seemed to rock on and on. I saw the other British soldier lying facedown and half-conscious, his musket inches from his outflung hands. I stumbled over toward him and picked up the heavy weapon. I needed it more as a staff than as a musket, though. I leaned on it, pushing myself upright. Then I tried to catch my breath and gather my wits at the same time. It was harder than it should have been.

"Forward, lads!" shouted a well-remembered voice behind me. "Out, out, and be smart about it! Follow me! Fortune favors the brave!"

Slow as a drunken snail, I swiveled around. Through the jagged five-foot-wide gap that ran from the ground to the roof of the jail bounded Lieutenant William Hunter, cutlass in hand, and behind him poured out a throng of armed men, all the condemned prisoners. Leaping over the smaller chunks of the wall, stepping around the larger, they pounded past me. I might as well have been invisible, for no one noticed me or gave so much as a glance at the musket I held.

They were all running down Lime Street toward the docks as fast as their legs could carry them. To me it was clear they were not just fleeing blindly from the jail: They had a goal in mind. I heard a Gaelic curse, and from the streaming smoke stumbled my uncle Patrick, carrying his black medical bag clutched to his chest.

"No one helps a man cumbered with a burden!" he raged as he went down on one knee to inspect the fallen soldier. The other one must have run off, for he was gone, though I had not noticed his leaving. For that matter, Abel Tate had vanished as well. Perhaps he had faded like the ghost he appeared to be, though I supposed he had merely joined the other running sailors. "Just a lump on the head," my uncle said, patting the groaning soldier's shoulder, though I doubted the man could hear him. "Fortunately, British soldiers have thick skulls, so you'll be all right in a day or two." An eddy of wind brought dust and smoke over both of us. He coughed and, without looking directly at me, said, "Come on, man, we must make haste!"

He didn't even recognize me, his own nephew, through all the dust. My ears still sang from the explosion, and before I could stir my wits to speak, my uncle had grabbed me by my collar and dragged me after him down the same way as the others. Still carrying that absurd musket, I staggered along behind, reeling as I did, for my sense of balance seemed to be astray. Only my uncle's death grip on my collar kept me moving. Once, I crashed into a shop front with my right shoulder, for the world seemed to be tilting, and a moment later I all but fell flat on my face, having taken a bad step.

"Use your land legs, man, if you don't wish to be left behind to hang!" urged my uncle, and at that he let go of my collar. Somehow I managed to stay on my feet, though the others steadily pulled away from me.

Behind us somewhere a bell began to clang frantically. I heard the booms of musket fire, but so far away that they could not have been aimed at us. More likely, it was the soldiers of Fort Charles alerting the town to the jailbreak. Alarmed citizens were peeking out of their doors, and then slamming them hard as they saw what was going on in the streets. Ahead of me, a soldier ran out from an alley, stared openmouthed at the mob of cutlass-swinging prisoners, and darted back again without firing a shot. My uncle was loping along ahead of me, but well to the rear of the pack, his long legs flashing. He was no more graceful than a racing stork would have been, but he did not slow down. He was leaving me behind.

The crowd of bellowing, cutlass-waving sailors

turned a corner, and I heard a crash and startled shouts. Moments later, I skidded around the corner myself, hopping on one foot, and saw a handcart on its side, dozens of big silvery fish spilled across the pavement. A scrawny man with eyes like saucers stood with his back pressed to a wall. "Blimey!" he exclaimed, his voice breathless. "Did you see those—" he broke off, staring at me and my borrowed musket. With a sorrowful wail, he threw both hands in the air. "I'm a poor man, sir! Spare my life, but take my fish!"

I was looking around, wild to see which way the sailors had run. "Why would I want your fish?"

"And why wouldn't you?" he snapped, all fear suddenly forgotten. "You sayin' there's something wrong with my fish? Quality folk come all the way from Spanish Town to buy my sea bass—"

Catching sight of the runaway prisoners, I ran off and left him standing there, waving a fish at me. We were at the docks by then, and snugged up to the nearest pier lay a trim one-masted sloop, tied bow and stern. "This way, lads!" came the faint voice of Lieutenant Hunter, and I saw men leaping from the dock to board the craft. Tate, or his ghost, chopped at the stern lines with his cutlass, and with wonderful speed, some of the other men raised the mainsail, which cracked as it caught the wind. "Come on, Patch!" urged the lieutenant. "Jump for it, man!" My uncle dived over the side of the vessel and landed on board like a thrown octopus, all boneless arms and legs.

I reached the pier, but already the bowline had been cut and the sloop was swinging out in the brisk breeze. A gangplank fell from the widening gap between ship and pier and splashed into the bay. Taking my courage in my hands, I started to murmur an Act of Contrition as I ran at top speed and leaped. Somehow or other my heels just cleared the larboard gunwale, and down I came with a thump and a thud, skidding across the deck and fetching up against the starboard gunwale with a shock that made me see spinning stars. Still, I murmured the last lines of the prayer: . . . "*occasiones proximas fugiturum. Amen.*"

For the moment I had no desire at all to rise, but half-lay and half-sat there, my mouth opening and shutting like that of a tarpon taken out of the water. I was in the shelter, if you could call it that, of a four-pound cannon.

"All here?" came Hunter's bellow. "Good! Mr. Adams, see to the larboard cannon! Gunners, to your posts! To quarters, to quarters, all! Step lively, lads, more speed and less talk from you all!"

"Cap'n!" shouted a sailor who was hanging in the shrouds. "The *Retribution* is making sail!"

From the docks, now behind us, came a quick, ragged rattle of musket fire. Looking up, I saw two holes punched in the triangular mainsail and felt, more than heard, the sounds: *Pock! Pock!* None of the other shots seemed to find a target at all. I thought surely it was the worst display of shooting I'd ever seen.

"Staysails!" shouted Hunter. "Make speed, men! Helmsman, make for the open sea! Mind the channel!"

"Aye, sir!" The helmsman was a sunburned sailor named Warburton, naked to the waist, grinning as he moved the tiller. He wore a long brown pigtail, and the wind whipped it in front of him like a pennant. At the bow, two triangular sails ran up, filled with wind, and cracked into taut curves.

More musket fire, so distant now that I doubted even a single ball could have reached the sloop. Finally I caught my wind and pulled myself up, leaning on that British musket. I looked wildly over the rail. Port Royal lay well to our stern. The crowds on the dock milled and moved in an excited way, but at that distance they looked no larger than so many ants. I saw that our sloop was fairly in the channel, making good speed, and that ahead lay the sea. But surely the threatening guns of Fort Charles would do for us, I thought. This was only a small craft, and one well-aimed thirty-two pound ball would sink us like a ship of lead.

"Cap'n Hunter," said Warburton the helmsman in a deep, musical booming voice, "*Retribution* drawin' up fast."

"Let Brixton come," returned Hunter with a loud and triumphant laugh. "The *Swift* is ours, and in an open sea with a quartering wind, we can outsail anything that lies in the harbor. Luff the mainsail, my hearties! Let him just try to catch us."

I looked back past the helmsman. The *Retribution* had spread its sails with remarkable speed, and she was barreling down the channel close behind us. Curves of white water leaped from her bows. To me, the frigate looked as if she were on the edge of leaving the water entirely and sailing through the air like something enchanted. I saw a puff of white smoke at her black bows, and fifty yards behind us the sea erupted in a fountain. I actually saw the dark blur of the cannonball skip like a thrown stone, flying another fifty yards to splash off to starboard before it sank.

Hunter leaped to the rail and stood on it, grasping a stay. "Oho! Fire away, Brixton, and waste your powder and shot! You can't hit us, you prize booby! Every decent gunner you had aboard is now here with me!"

We cleared the harbor entrance, and suddenly I realized what Hunter had done by luffing the sails. He had slowed our progress enough so that the *Retribution* had greatly closed the gap between us. The great cannons in Fort Charles lay silent, for they could not fire with the *Retribution* between us and the fort!

After something like two minutes had passed, the frigate's bow-chaser fired again, and this time I heard the boom an instant after I saw the smoke.

Again their shot went very wide, this time to larboard. The helmsman chuckled comfortably. "Never was very good at laying a gun, was old Brixton."

"Slow, too," observed Hunter. "Mr. Adams there can train a crew to fire off three accurate rounds in five minutes!"

Men stood expectantly by the lines, and others had swarmed up into the rigging. Across the deck from me, Mr. Adams was overseeing six men as they loaded and ran out the two four-pound cannons on that side.

"Stand by to go about," ordered Hunter over his shoulder, and men sprang to haul on the lines, obliging me to scoot back and out of their way. I stood with my hip pressed against the cannon carriage and stared like a lunatic at the drama on deck. Hunter did not seem to notice me at all as he put his hand to his mouth and called, "Adams, ready with the cannon! Chain shot, is it?"

"Aye, sir!" shouted Mr. Adams from the larboard rail across the deck from me. "Ready anytime!"

"Then we'll see if we can't trim Brixton's sails for him! Aim high, mind!"

"Aye, sir, high it is, and fire on the rise!" responded Adams.

"Helm alee!" shouted the captain, and the helmsman leaned on the tiller. The deck tilted sharply as the sloop heeled into the turn.

"Mainsail haul!" Hunter shouted, and then, "Fire as they bear, Mr. Adams!"

We tacked, the boom swung the mainsail from right to left, and the sail filled again, making the sloop leap forward as eagerly as a spirited horse. Beneath the boom I saw Adams standing between his two cannons, each one manned by three of the sailors. He raised his arm, held it for a second, and then dropped it suddenly.

Two gunners holding coils of burning slow match whipped the glowing ends down onto the cannons' touchholes, and both guns barked at once, a blast of white smoke blowing back over the rail. The cannons shot back in their slides, the whole little vessel shivered with the recoil, and as the smoke cleared, I saw sails dropping on the *Retribution*: Fore course, mainsail, and topgallants all came plunging down. It was an amazing amount of damage from two little four-pound guns. At that instant, the side of the navy ship vanished in a cloud of cannon smoke as she let loose a broadside.

Somehow—I had no notion how, at that range—she managed to miss us with every single shot, close as she had drawn. The balls ripped up the sea just astern of us, but never a hit did the *Retribution*'s gunners make. "Stand by to bring her about," Hunter ordered again.

By then the *Retribution* was between us and the next nearest fort, Fort Morgan, keeping us safe from their gunfire. But I thought Hunter must have gone wholly mad, for he swung the sloop in an arc that brought us close to the bows of the crippled navy ship. I could see Captain Brixton himself in the bows, shaking a fist our way. He lifted a speaking trumpet, and rolling across the waves I heard his outraged voice: "William Hunter! You're a renegade and a pirate, and I'll see you go to the bottom of the deep sea for this!"

"Not today, Mr. Brixton!" shouted back Hunter, with a deep laugh. "And from this day forth, it's Captain Hunter, if you please!" With a saucy wave, he dropped to the deck and gave the order to steer the sloop away from the *Retribution*.

The sloop was a nimble vessel that seemed to love a stiff gale, and the distance between the Royal Navy and us increased with surprising speed. For some little space there was nothing to break the silence but the crack of canvas, the creak of lines, and the rush of wind and wave.

Then the *Retribution* had just enough time to give us one parting broadside, rolling from the stern aft. It was no better aimed than the last, and not a single cannonball struck us. After that, her guns fell silent, I thought more from mere humiliation than from being out of range.

Someone touched my shoulder, making me leap a good foot into the air. I spun around to find myself staring into my uncle's wide green eyes. "You!" he exclaimed, sounding not at all pleased with our meeting. "I left word that you were to remain at the King's Mercy. What the devil are you doing aboard the *Swift*?"

"I—I—sir, I came to rescue you, sir!" I stammered.

"To rescue—you came to—why—what possibly possessed you to . . . ," sputtered my uncle, his green eyes wild with indignation. "And what in the name of all the saints in heaven are you doing standing there with a musket! Do you think you're playacting?" he demanded, snatching the weapon away and flinging it spinning overboard. "Pray God you have not killed someone with that thing!"

"No, sir, I have not!" I protested. "A soldier outside the Tabby House dropped it, and, and—and Abel Tate, who I saw being put over the side of the *Retribution* sewn up in canvas, somehow was there, and—and I picked up the musket, to have it to lean on, for the jail had blown up entirely, and there you were, and the soldier had a thick skull, you said, and you told me to follow you, and—" There I ran completely out of breath.

"That was you by the jail?" shouted my uncle. "I thought it was one of the men picking up the musket, in all that smoke and flying dust!" He raised his eyes to the cloudy gray heavens and moaned, "Oh, Kathleen, Kathleen, will ye never stop tormenting me?"

By that time I was thoroughly confused. "What does my mother have to do with this?"

He only shook his head. Behind us, Jamaica was fading in the haze and the distance. Ahead of us lay a rough gray sea, wind-streaked with foam.

And also ahead of us lay Lord only knew what fate.

CHAPTER TEN

Under the Jolly Roger

FOR A GOOD LONG TIME, everyone was far too busy with sailing the sloop and with other tasks to mind me at all. Men had dived into the hold of the ship, into the deckhouse, and had come running back with reports to Lieutenant—or now Captain—Hunter: "Water enough for a month, sir." "Good provisions, Cap'n, and lots of 'em." "Spare canvas and lines in top shape, Cap'n." "Ten round o' cartridge for each cannon already made up, sir. Plenty o' powder and shot more."

"Good," Hunter answered each time. Before long, a small crowd had collected in the stern, and raising his voice, Hunter addressed them:

"Everything's in order, then. The *Swift* is a fine, trim craft, and now all we have to do is treat her as she likes, my men. So let us turn to and escape from the bloody Royal Navy, eh?"

The men replied to this with a hearty burst of laughter.

With a grin, Mr. Hunter shouted, "Mr. Adams, you may raise our flag, if you please!"

"Aye, aye, sir!" returned Mr. Adams. He and another man attached a black bundle to a halyard. They hauled away with a will, and as it ran up to the masthead, the bundle broke out with a series of sharp snaps into piracy's own flag, the Jolly Roger. A white skull grinned on it, above a couple of crossed bones, which I supposed were meant to represent the long leg bones called femurs, though the resemblance was very faint. The men sent up a resounding cheer.

As for me, I was hanging onto the rail and still staring wildly about me. The weather was rapidly turning foul, with higher and higher winds whipping the white froth in long ghostly streamers from the tops of the steep, rolling gray waves, and the sloop bucked and plunged and twisted beneath a lowering sky of ragged dark clouds. Never had I been at sea in so small a craft, and the motion of it began to make my stomach lurch up and down.

Abel Tate came running toward the stern of the sloop and pulled up short to stare at me in evident surprise. His mouth opened and closed twice before he found a voice to speak with. "The doctor's nevvy, ain't ye?" he asked me. "Which ye was th' loblolly boy aboard o' the *Retribution*?"

I nodded. "I thought—but you were—Captain Brixton had a pistol—I saw you shot in the face, and—we buried you at sea!" I said, not making much sense even to myself.

Tate winked at me and chuckled comfortably. "Ah, well, ye see, in time I got better." Still laughing in a strange, gurgling fashion, he went past me to the stern and fell into conversation with Hunter, pointing at the sails and nodding at his captain's replies.

As for me, I had the strange, sick feeling that all my sense had been knocked out of me when the Tabby House blew up, and I had yet to recover a single particle of it. How could William Hunter so suddenly go from being a loyal subject of the king to being a turncoat, a renegade, and a pirate? And how in the name of every saint could my uncle Patrick, with all his learning and his nature, allow himself to be mixed up in such criminal doings?

And even more, why was everyone so—so *happy* about it all? Of the two dozen sailors aboard the *Swift*, every single one but me seemed to be larking about as if they were on holiday. The seamen wore big wide grins on their faces as they bent to their work or climbed into the rigging. Men sang as they hauled on lines, clapped one another on the back, threw their heads back and laughed long and loud at the stormy sky. It was as if life had become an enormous joke to them, one that I could not understand or crack even the slightest smile at.

My uncle had gone below deck, but he came back and went to talk to Hunter. In the veering wind, I could catch just a few snatches of what he was saying: ". . . no injuries, and that's a blessing . . . medical stores in good condition . . . hope your navigation is sound."

Then he turned and made his way over to me, hanging onto the rail because the deck was at a steep angle and bobbing up and down like a cork in a millrace. "This way," he said, taking hold of my arm and steering me forward along the deck and into the deckhouse.

This was a low structure in front of the mast. The fore part held the ship's galley, though the stove was cold at the moment. The aft part was divided into two neat cabins, and into one of these my uncle led me. "Sit," he said, his tone making it clear that the word was an order and not a request.

I sat hunched down in the one chair at the foot of a hanging cot, and he stood over me, stooping, for the ceiling was very low. He shook his head, his expression a mixture of sorrow and of anger, or so I thought. "Davy, Davy, Davy, now what am I to do with ye?"

"Me?" I asked, my temper rising in my voice. "Never mind about me at all. 'Tis yourself ye should be worried about, for when they catch you, they'll hang you, sure. I'm not the pirate, Uncle!"

"Oh ho. So you're no pirate, are ye?" asked my uncle with a lopsided grin. "And I am. Is that the way of it, then, you young fire-eater?"

I could not keep the hot fury from my tone: "All my life the English have looked down on me and made little of me just because I'm Irish, but for all that I'm still a loyal subject of King James! My own father fought in his army and died in his defense, and never in life would I turn my back on my country. But look at you! It's ashamed I am to call ye my last living relative, traitor that ye are!"

Uncle Patrick folded his arms across his chest and stared at me. He said in an even and serious way, "Traitor is a hard name to put to a man, Davy lad. You may think you know all about this affair, but—" He broke off, and then after a pause, he added, "It may be that you're not as sharp as a needle or as deep as a well, Davy. And it may well be that your Irish tongue and your Irish temper sometimes run right away with your wits, for you—"

"Patch?" It was Hunter's voice.

In a flash, Uncle Patrick hauled me up from my seat and shoved me behind him. "Quiet now for a spell, Davy," he whispered, and then he shouted, "In here, Hunter!"

Hunter stepped to the doorway of the cabin, though I could not see him from where I stood. I heard him say, "Well, Patch, you bloodthirsty old butcher, we've pulled it off!"

"Aye," said my uncle in a gloomy tone. "That we have, William Hunter."

"Then smile!" Hunter himself howled with laughter, like a madman. "We did 'em brown, Patch! Smooth as silk, right as rain! And the tale will be abroad in no time. There's not a soldier in Fort Charles who wouldn't love to send us to the bottom of the sea, and in a week's time you can wager your wig that the ships in Port Royal Harbor will have spread the news all across—"

Uncle Patrick took a half step to the left and dragged me from behind him. "Maybe things might have gone just a bit smoother, Hunter," he said.

Until that moment, I don't believe that Hunter had even suspected I had come aboard, though he might have seen me on deck at any time. He whistled a sharp note of surprise. "Davy!" He jerked his gaze to meet my uncle's. "Patch, I thought it was understood he was to be left at The King's Mercy. We agreed to that in the very beginning. Now, after all our plotting and planning, don't tell me you—"

"I did nothing!" said my uncle, cutting him off. "'Twas entirely his own notion to come and pay a social visit at the jail, and somehow, by hook or by crook, he got caught up in the turmoil, so he did."

Hunter, who had contrived somehow to remain as smooth-shaven in jail as aboard the *Retribution*, thoughtfully stroked his chin. "Well, now, this is a complication I did not look for," he said. "But then what's one more mouth to feed? And you'll still need a loblolly boy, after all. I suppose we could use him—"

"Don't be daft!" snapped Uncle Patrick. "That's clear out of the question, and you know it must be so. One of us has to have his head screwed on about this!"

"How much does he know?" asked Hunter, guardedly.

With decision, my uncle returned, "Nothing at all. I've told him not a word."

"Hmm." To me, Hunter said, "Davy, this is a pretty pickle. What in heaven's name did you mean, coming to the jail at that time of the morning?"

I bit down on my teeth, determined to tell this pirate nothing. I glared at him and simply shook my head, refusing to give him even a grunt by way of an answer.

Uncle Patrick grasped my shoulder and gave it a bit of a shake. "Mend your manners, nephew! Davy came to rescue me, it seems. Or to plead for my release, or to beg for mercy, or some such fool thing."

"Ah," said Hunter. "And then he just got caught up, as you say, in all the—"

"He picked up a bloody musket," growled my uncle. "And went charging through the streets of Port Royal with it, right at the tail of the crowd, just when the bell was ringing and all. Lord knows how many saw him."

Hunter puffed out his cheeks. "But you didn't tell him of our plans?" He paused for a moment, glanced at me, and then slowly continued, as though feeling his way: "To, ah, break out for a life as, ah, gentlemen of fortune, pillaging the ships along the Spanish Main?"

By now Uncle Patrick, whose fuse was always rather short, had flown into a passion of anger. "Hunter, am I the only one in this room with ears to hear? I have told you already, not a word to him did I speak of our plans, and not a word do I *intend* to speak of them now. Do you understand me, sir?"

Before Hunter could answer him, I drew myself up to my full height. Returning the man's gaze as coolly as I could manage, I snapped, "I don't want to hear the first word about your plans, sir—that, I don't!"

"Oh?" Hunter asked, with half a smile.

I was fuming. "Nothing you or my uncle can say to me can change my mind—*Lieutenant* Hunter! Ye need not worry about offering me a place or having an extra mouth to feed, for I'll not serve under the Jolly Roger, nor take orders from a pirate and a traitor!"

"You're the pirate," my uncle explained to Hunter. "I'm the traitor."

"Strong words, Davy," warned Hunter, the ghost of a smile still playing around his lips.

I caught my breath. "Mr. Hunter, I know you were sorely mistreated. Lord only knows, I thought Captain Brixton was a hard and bloody-minded taskmaster, and you were in the right of it when you defended Abel Tate, poor man. But the devil a shame have any of my family brought upon the name of Shea until this day, and the devil a bit will I add to the shame my uncle has now brought to it!

I'll never in all my life commit treason against the Crown, sir!"

"That was quite a speech," Hunter said slowly.

I started to say "thank you," but thought better of it. Still, it did seem to me to be a good speech, and I was proud of it, having just made it up on the spot.

To my uncle, Hunter said, "Where in heaven's name does this eloquence come from, Patch?"

"The fire in his speech comes from his sainted mother," said my uncle dryly. "And I'd bet my teeth that the nonsense comes from my late brother, who was loyal, true to the king, and the biggest fool ever to come out of Ireland."

Putting on a grave expression, Hunter said, "Well, David Shea, though a pirate I may be, as a man I can honor your feelings. You say you do not wish to serve under the pirate flag, nor do you wish to take orders from me. Very well. You will not have to do so."

"Good," I returned.

With a wink at my uncle, he said, "Shall we clap him in irons, then?"

"Into the hold," said Uncle Patrick decisively.

"No chains, though, for I despise the thought of chains and hate the memory of wearing them myself, and I would not do that to the boy. But I know there's a snug little cabin forward where we can keep this lad locked up tight, with perhaps a guard at the door to make sure he stays there. Conceivably that may keep him out of trouble until we can decide what we're going to do with him, once and for all."

"Do your worst," I said in what I hoped was a voice of scorn.

With a grin and a shrug, Hunter said, "So be it, then." He called over his shoulder for two men, told them what was to be done, and in less time than it takes me to write it, they had taken me below.

And so after that wild escape of all the rest of the prisoners, I found myself held captive in the bounding, tossing sloop-of-war *Swift*.

And, unlucky me, the very moment the sailors had locked me into the dark little cabin, for the first time in my life I was violently and thoroughly seasick.

Aurora Awaits

FOR THE BEST PART OF three days I lay in the cubbyhole, sick to the point of not caring whether I lived or died. Some sailor had cleaned the deck after my first horrible round of seasickness, and another had considerately brought me a pail for the second. After I had thrown up everything in my stomach, I lay, or tried to lie, in my cot, but the sea tossed the *Swift* terribly. The storm was heavier than any I had experienced before. The *Swift* rose and fell, tossed and bucked and plunged more like a mad horse than a proper ship. Except eventually a horse got tired. The *Swift* didn't.

Finally, though, the wind blew itself out, the sea

gradually grew smoother, and I began to feel as if I might just possibly survive. On the first calm day, Abel Tate himself, alive and all, brought me some soft-tack—ordinary bread, I mean, not the ship's biscuit called hardtack. Once I had taken a careful nibble of it, I found myself ravenous with hunger. I ate heartily and drank great gulps of water. Not long after that, I asked for, and received, a lantern, and at last I could get a good look at my berth, or my prison.

The cabin was better than I had supposed it to be during my long hours of seasickness in the dark. The bed was a hanging cot, narrow but comfortable enough for someone of my size. I figured the compartment must lie forward, for the wall curved inward, as if it were the point where the ship's bows began. And though the berth was but a small nook, it was clean enough. About noon on that first calm day, I heard the gruff voice of the sailor guarding the door, curiously loud and distinct: "Welcome, your honor. 'Tis a fine life, bein' a pirate, and as it were all your idea, I thanks ye, I does."

And quite as loudly, my uncle's voice answered him: "Sure, and we shall make the decks of our enemies run red with their own blood before we're through!" There followed a burst of hearty laughter, and then came the briefest rattle of key in lock. The door swung outward to reveal Uncle Patrick.

"Have you come to kill me?" I asked, very coldly. "I mean, as you've turned traitor and pirate?"

His face grew red, but he spoke in an even, quiet tone. "And a good morning to you, too, Gerald," he said.

"Gerald?" That was my father's name.

"Oh, so now you're Davy again. That's well, though it was nice to hear my dear brother's voice again. You had his self-righteousness down pat. But never mind that. What I've come to tell you is this: Now that you are feeling better, neither William nor I want to confine you in this hole all the blessed day and night. If you'll cut no capers, you can have some freedom in the daytime, though we'll have to lock the door at night, to be sure. And to begin with, if you are agreeable, you may take the air with me now, if you've a mind to."

Faith, it was an attractive offer, for I was tired of lying on the cot. "What do I have to do in return?"

My uncle spread his hands. "Only give me your

word, or your parole, as the French say, that you will not try to interfere with the working of the sloop."

I thought that over and tipped him a short nod. Not that he had convinced me, truly. 'Twas rather that I had no notion of any way to interfere, even if I wanted to. He led me up a ladder and onto the deck. It was a dazzling day, and for some moments, my eyes could see almost nothing. But as they became used to the sun again, I saw Captain Hunter, as he now called himself, on the quarter-deck, taking a sight on the sun with his cross-staff. "Make it noon, Mr. Adams," he said.

"Noon it is, sir," replied Mr. Adams, and he rang the ship's bell. This all made me feel very odd, for the ritual of "shooting the sun" was one I had seen every day aboard the *Retribution*, when Hunter was still an honorable officer.

Hunter caught sight of me and gave me a jaunty wave, the villain. To Adams, he announced, "I'm going aloft for a quick look around for likely prizes." He swung on a line from the quarterdeck to the rail, and then scurried up the shrouds to the top. Watching him, you would never have guessed that mere months ago he had been wounded and near death.

"Come," my uncle said to me, and he led me back to the steps leading up from the gun deck to the quarterdeck. We climbed these, and I walked to the stern and looked back over the taffrail at the *Swift*'s wake, a paler blue traced on the nearly indigo face of the sea. Bobbing along behind us was the captain's barge. Despite its impressive name, it actually was only a small rowboat or dinghy, into which six or at a pinch eight sailors might fit. A canvas cover stretched over it, to keep the waves out, I supposed, and it trailed along like a small, frisky dog.

"Heads up, if you please, Mr. Adams!"

Something black like an oblong ball fell lightly from the yardarms. I looked up just in time to see the captain spring from the yardarm to a backstay and slide down it to the deck.

Mr. Adams caught the black ball and snapped it out, revealing a white skull and crossed bones before he folded it up. Hunter had struck the Jolly Roger, and now the *Swift* flew no flag at all. Adams smiled wickedly at me "'Tis in order to sneak closer to ships the captain intends to plunder or take."

Hunter reached the quarterdeck, dropping down as lightly as one of the midshipmen, and gave me a mocking smile. "Good to see you up and about, young Shea. I assume you are hungry after your recent indisposition. Pray join your uncle as my guest."

"Bread and water is more suited for a prisoner, sir!"

Uncle Patrick gave me a quick shake. "Manners, Davy! Come, we are being friendly, but we have to make some settlement about you."

I might have protested more, but they did outnumber me. And I was hungry, Lord knows.

The *Swift*'s aft cabin was tiny by comparison with that of the *Retribution*, but the sloop did boast a double row of windows, all of them swiveled open for coolness' sake. Hunter's great table could seat no more than four, and in truth even three of us were crowded. The food, though, was really good. We had a mutton pie, soft-tack in plenty, with butter, boiled cabbage, new potatoes, and the kind of pudding called plum duff. Even after my first breakfast in several days, I had the appetite of a wolf, and for many minutes I turned all my attention to the food.

"Sure, you must be on the mend," Uncle Patrick observed. "Now, here's what we plan for you. The hurricane has blown us clean into the Bahamas. Word of our escape cannot possibly have reached so far in such a short time. Captain Hunter now proposes to hail the first westbound British merchant vessel we sight—"

"And plunder it, I'm sure," I said, laying down my fork.

My uncle's face turned red. "No, you young dog. And put you aboard her, is what, and I will pay—*pay*—your passage back to Port Royal, where you *will* stay with the good Mrs. Cochran until I can provide her with more exact instructions about what is to be done with you. She already holds a sum of money from me that should keep you for a year, provided you do not eat every day as you have done here."

I crossed my arms. "And how will you even get close enough to hail a ship? Surely any in these waters will be wary of a strange sail."

Hunter chuckled easily. "We're too small a craft, with our eight little popgun cannons, to look much of a threat. And I shall fly a British flag, of course."

"Another crime, Mr. Hunter?" I asked. "Sailing under false colors, I mean."

With a short laugh, Hunter said, "Indeed, I had not thought of that! Mark it down, Patch! Mutiny, jailbreak, piracy, kidnapping, false colors . . . an impressive list!"

"Saints above us, but the two of you will drive me mad!" exclaimed my uncle. "If you've finished eating a week's worth of provisions, Davy, leave us. But be careful of the crew, for they've half a mind to feed you to the sharks!"

I stood hesitantly. "You're not going to throw me in chains, then?"

Hunter chuckled. "I am not. You cannot escape while we are at sea and clean out of sight of land. But because we're fighting a foul wind, I will have you locked in your berth at night, when you might be a trouble to the working of the sloop."

I left them and went out onto the deck. The sky had cleared since the storm and was a deep blue. The sailors paid me no mind at all but shouted and laughed and seemed excessively hearty. I roamed forward and looked all round the horizon, but never the shadow of land could I spy. At last I went below again, and outside the little compartment that was my prison, I noticed two things. One was that the padlock on the door was a heavy one, as big as the palm of my hand.

But the other was that the three hinges that held the door in place were on this, the outer side. I pressed on the bottoms of the pins that held these hinges in place, and found they slipped up and down very easily. I had no doubt that the sailors had oiled them, for they were forever taking care of little things like that aboard the sloop.

I had the glimmer of an idea, but to make it work, I needed to begin with some preparation. And the likeliest place, I thought, might be the ship's galley.

"What d'you want?" asked George Bowles, a burly sailor who was the *Swift*'s acting cook.

"Please, sir," I said, trying to sound humble, "I came to see if there is some task I could do for you. In payment, like, for my passage."

Bowles stared at me, pulling his lower lip. "Well . . . I s'pose ye might wash the pots an' pans an' such."

In no time, I stood at a slopping basin of salt

water, scrubbing away with handfuls of sand. Whenever Mr. Bowles looked away, I pocketed a few things I needed.

Before long, I was back in my berth, using a small knife, with a blade only three inches long, to whittle away at a short piece of kindling wood. I had slipped out the middle pin from the hinges of my door, and I used it to judge how thin to whittle the wood. I meant to cut only two wooden pins, not three, and make them short, at that. Even with the small knife, it did not take long. I carefully gathered the shavings so that no one might find them and ask what I was up to.

Three times I slipped out to check the fit. Once a sailor was coming along the passageway and I had to go back, but the last time, I removed first the top hinge pin, replacing it with a wooden one, and then the bottom one, putting another wooden one there. I tried the door. It still opened, though it wobbled a bit. I did not think that there, in the darkness, anyone would notice the change, and I trusted that the motion of the ship would keep anyone from noticing that the door opened unsteadily now.

I was all set. I put the three metal pins in my pocket, went on deck and tossed the shavings over the side, and settled in to wait until we were within reach of land.

Over the next days we worked steadily to the south and east, but a strong wind was in our very teeth. Of course, a sailing ship could not go directly toward the wind, so we had to tack, zigging ten miles to the east and then zagging ten to the south. Changing the sails meant that most of the men had to be on deck, and that was just what I wanted.

At last we made a landfall, toward dusk. I climbed the shrouds to catch a glimpse of a low, green island, still distant. The wind continued foul, so the *Swift* would have to beat to and fro all night to work in and anchor.

At sunset, they locked me in my cabin. I waited for three or four hours, until I heard the bosun's whistle call, "All hands," and then the patter and clatter of feet on the deck. This was my chance.

I braced my back against the bulkhead, or wall, and my feet against the inner corner of the door and pushed hard, and harder still. I felt more than heard the crack as the wooden pin broke off, and the door pivoted on the top hinge and the padlock. I put my shoulder against it and hit it once, twice, three times, and the top pin cracked in two. I just managed to catch and hold the door to keep it from falling with a crash. I opened it, using the padlock as the hinge, and then carefully replaced it. Hurriedly, I dug the hinge pins from my pocket and pushed them all into their hinges. That would leave a pretty puzzle for Mr. Hunter, I thought. Let him try to discover how I had melted through a locked door!

I crept back along the passageway to the stern, taking care to press into dark corners whenever I heard a footstep or a voice. I made my way into the stern cabin, empty since all hands were on deck. The stern windows were still open, and through them a providential moon gave me some light. I squirmed through one of the windows, a tight fit even for me, and crouched on a sort of narrow ledge beside the rudder, hearing the wash of the sea beneath me.

Then I froze, for from the deck, mere feet above my head, came the voices of my uncle and of Mr. Hunter.

"Don't fret yourself, Patch," Hunter said to some remark of my uncle's that I had not caught. "Sometimes you have to have a little faith. Besides, the *Aurora* is worth the wait. The French can't sail worth a tinker's curse, but they build sweet."

My uncle seemed to be in a bad mood as he snapped, "First we have to take the faithless jade, and to do that she has to be there to take. And you know who we have to depend on for that!"

Soothingly, Hunter answered, "That's where the faith comes in. Once we have the *Aurora*, the problem of your nephew will solve itself."

"Saints, I'm not so certain of that," shot back Uncle Patrick. "Davy is an ingenious lad, and he can cause more trouble than you may suspect."

"Nonsense," said Hunter with a laugh. "We take the *Aurora*, take on the new crew, and leave the *Swift* for the loyal officers. The boy will return to Port Royal in her, and Mrs. Cochran will know what to do. . . ."

I had heard enough. In the moonlight I could see the captain's barge still towing along behind us. Taking a deep breath, I let myself drop into the sea.

The splash was shockingly loud to me, and salt

water stung my nose and my eyes, but I was a good swimmer. I kicked back to the surface, took a gasp of air, and bobbed up high enough to grab the towline. I let myself slide back along it until I could climb into the rowboat, slipping under the canvas cover. It was dry enough there, and I lay catching my breath. The water and air were both blood heat, and I felt no chill at all, though to be sure I shivered a little.

It must have been past midnight when I heard again Hunter's voice, this time fainter, for I was farther away. Still, what he said was clear enough: "I see her, at single anchor. The *Aurora*, for certain. I'd recognize those tall masts anywhere. We'll close in with her by dawn. Then hoist the black flag and away!"

I peeked out. Low as I was, I could see the dark bulk of the island, only two or three miles away, and I thought I could make out the lights of a ship. That must be the vessel, I thought, that my uncle and Hunter were planning to steal. Still, the wind was against us, and it would take at least three hours for Hunter to work in close enough to attack. That gave me time. Using the small knife, I began to saw through the towline of the dinghy. It was tough work, but at last the rope gave, and with a little lurch the rowboat drifted free. I hoped no one would glance back at the barge, at least not for a time.

The *Swift* sailed on, her stern lanterns and top lights shrinking with surprising speed. I threw off the canvas cover and broke out two oars from where they were stored beneath the seats. Then I began to row toward the island, and toward the mysterious *Aurora*.

Very quickly I discovered that the wind had some effect on the rowboat, too, and that a wicked current wanted to sweep me clean past the island. But I adjusted the direction and the speed of my rowing, and made slow progress. Out in the dark, the *Swift* would be tacking again, coming in to make her landfall. If only I could hold out to keep rowing, I could just beat her.

It seemed like I rowed forever. I felt blisters rising on the palms of my hands, and my shoulders began to ache drearily from the effort. But the island grew, as each glance back over my shoulder told me, and before long I was sure of the ship that lay under its shelter. At one point I had to wrestle the rowboat through a line of breakers, where a sandbar must have lurked, and I thought I would be capsized. Indeed, I shipped enough water to sink the boat had it been any more heavily loaded, but somehow it wallowed through into calmer water, and I hastily bailed quarts and gallons of seawater out.

Finally, the *Aurora* loomed over me, a beautiful, sleek craft. In the moonlight I could see her cannon ports, a full row of them, and I counted fourteen to the one side. "Ahoy, the ship," I tried to shout, but my voice was hoarse and rusty.

Twice more I called, but I had actually bumped the rowboat's nose against the frigate's side before I was answered with a peevish, "What boat is that?"

"Please, sir," I shouted back, "I'm only a boy, and all alone, and need help coming aboard."

A lantern bobbed about on the deck above me. I heard a mutter of voices, and then the sailor called back down, "Hold where ye are, and I'll come to ye."

A rope snaked down from the deck, and a moment later a thin man slid down it, dropping into the dinghy and swearing as he got his feet wet. "You've pretty well swamped this craft," he observed accusingly.

"I did my best," I croaked.

"Well, can ye climb?" he came back, still not impressed by my seamanship.

"Faith, and I'm that weary with rowing, I cannot," I confessed.

"Well, well, here, let me take a hitch." He quickly tied the rope around me. Then he shouted up, "Haul away, there!"

I felt myself plucked right out of the boat and swung up and over the rail, and a moment later, plop, I was on the deck. The lantern was behind the two figures who had hauled me aboard. I could see them only as dark shapes. "Pardon, gentlemen," I panted from my knees, for I had dropped to them as the rope dumped me down, "but may I speak to the captain?"

"Which this is 'im 'ere," the thinner of the two silhouettes said.

I turned to the other. "Pray, sir, are you truly the captain?"

And to my shock, the other replied with a laugh,

"Well, Davy Shea, if I'm not, then this French tub doesn't have one!"

He reached behind him for the lantern, and in its yellow light, I found myself staring up into the face of Sir Henry Morgan.

CHAPTER TWELVE

How I Turned Pirate

"B-BUT—YOU—I—"

Morgan offered me a hand and pulled me to my feet. "Well, don't stand there stammering, you young whelp! Speak your mind. I don't propose to remain here all night."

I licked my lips, realizing how dry all that rowing had made me. "Sir," I said in my frog-croak of a voice, "I came here to warn you that your ship is about to be attacked by pirates!"

"Pirates?" thundered Morgan. "By the Powers, pirates, you say! Name 'em, the dirty dogs!"

I shook my head. "No, sir. At least, if I do, I want a favor from you, so I do. And remember that when none of the surgeons in Port Royal could bring you relief or ease, my uncle could. Have a thought for him!"

"Your uncle is a renegade, Davy," Morgan said in a level voice. "He's been declared an outlaw, and every honest man's hand will be raised against him. Wait, though: Is it your uncle and that villain Hunter who are about to attack us? Thunder, I think that must be the case! And are they still in that neat little sloop they stole?"

"Please, sir," I said, shaking with exhaustion and worry and fear. "Their ship is small—"

"It is not a ship!" yelled Morgan, making me flinch. "A ship has three masts, all square-rigged! A sloop is not a ship!"

"Their *sloop* is badly armed, and they haven't many men," I went on doggedly. "If you fire your cannon—not to blow them out of the water, but just to show that you're on to them—they'll surely haul away. Please, sir, Uncle Patrick may be a renegade, but he is my uncle!"

Morgan stroked his beard. "And you've thought all this out, have you?"

"No, sir, I'm making it up as I go along," I confessed.

Morgan threw back his head and roared with laughter, though I saw nothing funny at all in what I had said. Suddenly he held the lantern closer and whistled. "Boy, you've torn your hands to ribbons!"

I held out my palms. They were a sight, blistered and bloody-raw. "I am not used to rowing miles through the ocean," I told him.

"Sloop coming in under plain sail," a sailor called from the maintop.

"Shiver my timbers," growled Morgan. "You're a rare plucked 'un, so ye are. I always said the Irish had hearts in their bellies! That will be the *Swift*. Well, let's wait and see what they offer us, shall we?"

The sun was just below the horizon by that time, the east growing lighter. The *Swift* came gliding silent in to the anchorage, slanting against the breeze, and struck her sails a few yards from us. Still, the craft drifted closer, until I heard Hunter order the anchors to be dropped. They went down with a splash, and the *Swift* rocked to a stop hardly two yards away from the hull of Morgan's ship.

Morgan gripped my shoulder with his huge hand. "Stand steady, lad," he warned. "Let's see if we can surprise them." Then he made a noise in his throat that I took to be a snarl but sounded suspiciously like a chuckle.

A moment later grapples flew over the rail, caught a grip, and then half the crew of the *Swift* climbed hand over hand up the boarding ropes and dropped quiet as death onto the deck. In the ruddy light of dawn, Hunter's expression as he saw me was one of shock and astonishment. "How did you—?"

"This lad has told me all about your plans, you pirate," boomed Morgan. "Is Patch aboard?"

Hunter turned and held his hand to his mouth. "Patch! Here's the devil of a thing!"

"What is it?" bawled my uncle from the deck of the *Swift*.

Morgan pushed me to the rail. "'Tis myself, Uncle," I shouted.

I could see my uncle's startled face. "Davy? What the blazes? Hunter, you long fool, you told me that door was locked! Saints save us all! Stay where you are, Davy! I'll climb up—"

"Throw the doctor a line," ordered Morgan, "or we'll have to fish him out of the bay. The man can't climb worth spit." A sailor tossed the end of a rope to my uncle, he made it fast around his middle, and up he was hauled like a sack of dried peas.

When he had been brought onto the deck, he stared at me with his eyes bulging. "Your door is locked," he said. "We checked it not long past midnight."

"And your barge is still towing behind, no doubt," said Morgan dryly to Hunter. "Or could that be the craft in which this lad rowed across miles of water to prove his loyalty to King James? Bless my soul, I believe it is!"

"Davy, why did you do this?" asked Uncle Patrick. "Just give me a reason—any reason will do—so when I reach heaven's gates your sainted mother won't hurl me down to torment!"

Morgan clapped my shoulder. "I told you! He's a sailor of the king, so he is, and he came to me at great risk to warn me of your treacherous attack. Bedad, he stood here like a man and made a stirring plea that I spare your cowardly lives!"

"I did?" I whispered.

"That you did, lad. Handsomely done, too, and very brave you were," said Morgan.

"Treacherous attack?" asked Hunter, sounding as if he were a few steps behind all of this. My uncle merely stared up at the heavens, shaking his head.

"Blast my eyes, you traitorous scum! Don't you know there are rules to these affairs? You can't attack a ship if it doesn't have a crew to fight against, can you?" asked Morgan. He bellowed lustily, "All hands on deck! Lively, lads! Stir your stumps!"

And the hatches of the *Aurora* fairly erupted with a stream of men. Sailors, none of them young, all of them scarred, came pouring onto the deck. Some had but one eye, some but one hand, and three or four stamped along on peg legs. Their hair and beards were gray, and many of their grins were all but toothless, but they came in an almost silent, disciplined wave.

To their credit, my uncle and the captain of the *Swift* stood their ground, though I was grieved at heart, knowing they would be arrested and hanged. Or would Morgan make them walk the plank, as befitted pirates?

"A hundred and ninety men," Morgan said. "Some of 'em battered and some of 'em stove in, but sounder hearts never sailed the seas, no, nor braver ones, neither! Picked 'em out myself, from the cream of my old crews. They might not look like much, but they know how to fight—hey, my hearties?"

And suddenly that whole crowd of dangerous-looking men was brandishing cutlasses. They sent up a cheer that echoed back from the shore.

"I see," said Hunter.

"Ye grasp the situation, do ye?" said Morgan with a white grin.

"Indeed, Sir Henry."

Morgan nodded. "Then what d'ye propose to do, William Hunter?"

Hunter drew his own cutlass. "I propose to take your ship and your crew, Sir Henry, and set out a-pirating!"

"You do, do you?"

"Aye, sir, I do!"

There was a fearful pause as they glared at each other. Until Sir Henry shrugged.

"Oh, right, then. Better get on with it." Morgan turned and faced the massed villains who had come on deck at his call. "Lads, three cheers for your new captain!"

Both the crews, the one from the *Swift* and the one from the *Aurora*, shouted out three cheers and began to slap one another on the back. I stood stunned. Above the din, Morgan yelled, "Patch, you'd better look to this scamp's hands, for he's fair ruined them on those oars. Come on into the cabin."

"But I don't understand!" I babbled to my uncle.

"Faith, and why should today be different from any other day?" he asked dryly.

We went back into a stern cabin even grander than the *Retribution* had boasted. Patch looked at Morgan, shook his head, and said, "You seem to be feeling better yourself, Sir Henry."

Morgan laughed. "I needed a plank under my boots, and salt water under that, is all! By the Powers, I feel ten years younger. I wish I could go with you lads—that, I do."

Uncle Patrick shook his head at the state of my hands. He dressed the raw spots and said, "'Tis a foolish lad ye are, and glad I'll be when you're safe in Port Royal again, to be sure."

"Hold hard there," said Morgan. "Young Davy can't go back. There's a man swearing blue fire that he robbed him at gunpoint of ten guineas and some fish, and half the town saw him running through the streets with a musket, covering your escape."

"That tears it!" shouted my uncle. "Davy, you've pitched headfirst into more trouble than ye can handle!"

"Come, Patch, it's none so bad as that," said Morgan. He unlocked a desk and took from it some papers. "Captain Hunter, as the king's confidential agent, I present you with these letters of marque and reprisal. Consider yourself on detached duty aboard His Majesty's hired vessel *Aurora*. You're to rid these waters of pirates, especially of Jack Steele—"

"I don't understand!" I wailed again.

"'Tis a scheme," my uncle said, barely containing his temper. "'Tis a scheme of my own making, Lord help me, a full payment for playing Follow the Fool with an old pirate!"

Morgan shook with laughter. "But it was a grand idea, Patch, my lad!"

Uncle Patrick spun on him with an angry snarl. "'Twas a flight o' fancy to occupy us during a bloodletting!"

"Aye," agreed Morgan. "Ye see, Davy, I'm enough

of a rogue myself to operate just on the edge of the law. If I were younger, I'd have done this job myself. Your uncle and I dreamed it all up one day months ago: Equip a ship, man it with pirates, and send it out to find Jack Steele. I'm too old for that kind of caper, and so I thought that was the end of it. But Patch found Hunter here, a good officer and a true one, and my old friend Captain Brixton agreed to the plan. We've set Mr. Hunter up to look like a pirate. Now, ye've heard the old saying, 'Set a thief to catch a thief'?"

And then I began to see his meaning. "If everyone thinks Mr. Hunter is a pirate," I said slowly, "then he might be able to get close enough to capture Jack Steele!"

"'Tis playacting," said my uncle, "but playacting in dead earnest. We'll sail about, and we'll take enemy ships where we can—Spanish, French, and Dutch privateers that prey on English ships. And we will wait for the chance to take the big prize, the *Red Queen*."

"Or to blow her out of the water, and Jack Steele with her!" said Hunter.

Morgan put in, "Only King James and I know

that Captain Hunter now has legal papers allowing him to pose as a pirate and stop Jack Steele. And this is the ship and the crew to do it. The *Aurora* is solid, French built and British taken, with twenty-eight nine-pound cannons and plenty o' stores. I'll vouch for the crew. They're no beauties, that they are not, but they're true as steel and brave as lions."

"I thought Mr. Hunter's men seemed too—too jolly, somehow. And yet I never guessed 'twas all in play," I said. "Am I that stupid?"

Morgan clapped me on the back. "If ye are, then so are all the sharpest men in Port Royal—for we pulled the wool over all their eyes, so we did!"

The door swung open, and Abel Tate peeked into the cabin. Finally understanding, I said, "Captain Brixton only pretended to shoot Abel Tate, there—"

"To make the mutiny more lifelike," said Hunter. "We sewed up some rolls of canvas in a hammock, and that was what was thrown overboard. We took Abel ashore on a stretcher, with his face covered, and no one was the wiser."

Abel grinned, and I said to him, "But you were whipped—surely Captain Brixton didn't—"

Tate laughed from the doorway. "Nay, lad, it

didn't hurt. The cat-o'-nine-tails was made o' felt, dipped in pig's blood, to make it seem as if I were bleeding. But didn't I sound good? It's playacting I should be! And later, who brought the gunpowder round to blow up the old Tabby House? Who else but me?" He touched a knuckle to his forehead and said, "Askin' your pardon, sirs, but may we begin makin' the switch between the two vessels?"

"Make it so," Hunter ordered, and Tate left us, closing the door behind him.

My uncle turned to Morgan. "Sir Henry, perhaps you could take my nephew to Barbados or—"

"No, sir," said Sir Henry promptly. "Take him somewhere that he knows no one? Fie, Patch! Your nephew belongs aboard this ship. He's a lad with pluck and courage, and maybe he can get some sense knocked into his Irish skull. At any rate, he's too well known. Patch, you have yourself a loblolly boy."

The rest of the morning passed in a whirl. Morgan and a skeleton crew went across into the *Swift*. Hunter took command of the *Aurora*. Well before noon, the *Swift* weighed anchor and headed out to sea. Morgan, standing at the rail, waved.

"Fare you well, Sir Henry," Hunter called.

"I shall tell everyone in Port Royal how gallant you were!" Morgan shouted back. "An act of generosity, merely taking my ship and leaving me this one to return in! But I'll inform Governor Molesworth you're a desperate band and that you hurl defiance in his teeth! That will make him shake in his boots!" And the old buccaneer threw back his head and roared.

Long before the *Swift* had vanished from sight, Captain Hunter—for he was indeed a captain now, commanding his own ship, lawfully— ordered the *Aurora* to make for the open sea. The anchor came up. The men rose into the shrouds, loosed the sails, and the great frigate began to lean toward the horizon.

I stood in the bows, beside my uncle, who seemed dangerously quiet. "Don't be angry with me," I said. "Faith, if you had told me the truth at the beginning—"

"I am in no mood to argue, Davy," he said shortly. "Perhaps I could send you back to your Mr. Horne in England—"

I nodded. "Aye, but that would mean it would

take me longer to return to sea. And I would, you know. No matter where you and Captain Hunter sail, somehow I would find you again, and I'd simply creep aboard your ship. I have the shame of betraying you to work off my conscience!"

My uncle gave me a crooked grin, and then burst into his creaking laughter. "Saints preserve me, Davy, but you're going to be a man to reckon with, if ye manage to grow up at all. Lad, you stood up for what you believed in, and did a brave job of it. Can't you see you did everything *right?* Your father would be proud of you this day." He sniffed and then growled, "I know I am."

"Then I can stay?"

"You stay. You're going to have adventures to tell your grandchildren, if you live through this." He creaked a little more, and then said, "You've beaten me, lad, fair and square. All right, then, from this moment, we're shipmates! But you're the one for honesty and for gallantry and for serving your king and country, so I wonder about one thing: Now tell me, Davy Shea, how does it feel to be a pirate?"

I considered this. "It feels just fine, sir."

And so it did.

Pirate Hunter 1: Mutiny!

Much of this book is based on truth. The golden age of piracy in the Caribbean began in the 1600s. Spain claimed all of the West Indies, Central America, and most of South America. In the opinion of the king of Spain, no other nations had any right to send ships to these areas.

But the Spanish settlers in the colonies did not want to pay the high prices that Spain charged for goods and supplies. The colonists eagerly traded with Portuguese, French, Dutch, and English ships. To the authorities in Spain, these were pirate vessels. The traders, though, thought they were performing a service for the colonies and making a living for themselves.

On the island of Tortuga, north of what is today Haiti, a group of tough cattle drovers sprang up in the early 1600s. These men hunted wild cattle or raised and slaughtered domesticated cattle to provide meat for the Spanish and other sailors. Because they smoked the meat on frames called boucans, these men, mostly French, became known as boucaniers. The English called them buccaneers. When English leaders like Sir Henry Morgan set out to make war against the Spanish, they recruited these rough buccaneers as soldiers. Morgan was a privateer himself. He had a commission from the governor of Jamaica that allowed him to fight the enemies of the king of England, including the Spanish.

But the Spanish considered Morgan and his buccaneers pirates, of course. By the time of our story, 1687, Spain had signed treaties with the French, Dutch, and English. As part of the treaty agreements, the governments were supposed to disband the buccaneer groups. Many of these men had grown accustomed to their plundering way of life, and they had no intention of changing. The difference was that, without their governments' permission to attack Spanish ships and colonies, now the buccaneers were outlaws. These were the true pirates. Even Sir Henry Morgan, an old buccaneer himself, worked to hunt down these pirates and to bring peace to the West Indes.

It took many years. The high point of piracy in American waters was between the late 1680s and about 1740. The names of the pirates of that time are still well known: Calico Jack Rackham, Anne Bonney and Mary Reade (two women pirates!), Major Stede Bonnet, Captain William Kidd, and of course Edward Teach— Blackbeard. Our Jack Steele is a little like them. He is different, too, because most American pirates sailed small vessels, sloops or brigs, and were loners. Jack Steele, a natural leader, sails a mighty warship and is seeking to become the Pirate King of the New World.

So although our tale is fiction, it has roots in the truth. Piracy was not a fun occupation. It was dangerous, cruel, and dirty, and most pirates had short careers and short lives. Still, they were men who liked freedom and who hated the life of ordinary sailors. A Royal Navy sailor could expect bad food, hard work, and whippings for every mistake or every minor violation of a rule. Their pay was often months or even years late in coming. And merchant sailors had it even worse! At least a Royal Navy captain usually gave no more than one or two dozen lashes as punishment. A private captain could order any number. Some of them forced sick men to climb the rigging and work the sails, even though the effort sometimes killed the suffering sailors. When we read about such true stories and thought about the pirates of the West Indies, it seemed to us that the strange thing was not that honest sailors sometimes turned pirate. Odder still was that most of them did not!

Welcome to the world of pirates and pirate hunting. It is a rugged world, and it does not have much glamour in it. But it offers excitement and adventure, and even humor of a kind. We hope you enjoy the voyage!

—Brad Strickland and Thomas E. Fuller
FEBRUARY 2002

BRAD STRICKLAND has written or cowritten nearly fifty novels. He and Thomas E. Fuller have worked together on many books about Wishbone, TV's literature-loving dog, and Brad and his wife Barbara have also written books featuring Sabrina, the Teenage Witch, the mystery-solving Shelby Woo, and characters from *Star Trek*. On his own, Brad has written mysteries, science fiction, and fantasy novels. When he is not writing, Brad is a Professor of English at Gainesville College in Oakwood, Georgia. He and Barbara have a daughter, Amy, a son, Jonathan, and a daughter-in-law, Rebecca. They also have a house full of pets, including two dogs, three cats, a ferret, a gerbil, and two goldfish, one named George W. Bush and one named Fluffy.

THOMAS E. FULLER has been co-authoring young adult novels with Brad Strickland for the last five years. They are best known for their work on the Wishbone mysteries as well as a number of radio dramas and published short stories. Otherwise, Thomas is best known as the head writer of the Atlanta Radio Theatre Company. He has won awards for his adaptation of H. G. Wells' "The Island of Dr. Moreau," his original drama, "The Brides of Dracula," and the occult western, "All Hallow's Moon." Thomas lives in Duluth, GA, in a slightly shabby blue house full of books, manuscripts, audio tapes and too many children including his sons Edward, Anthony, and John and occasionally his daughter, Christina.

READ ON FOR A PREVIEW OF THE NEXT
ADVENTURES OF CAPTAIN HUNTER AND
THE CREW OF THE AURORA IN

The Guns of Tortuga

"MAKE READY, MY LADS. Make ready!" rang out a laughing voice. Captain William Hunter stood next to the helmsman and the whipstaff, legs spread, hands on hips, head thrown back. We had been operating as pirates for nearly five months, but his appearance still seemed most strange to me. Gone was the elegant officer of His Majesty's Royal Navy that Sir Henry Morgan had recruited. In his place was the most piratical-looking fellow north of the Spanish Main.

William Hunter was resplendent in a long emerald-green coat with red frogs and piping. His blouse and pants gleamed white, separated by the yellowest silk sash its owner could find. And where he had found his hat with the ostrich plumes was still a mystery. Mr. Adams, the second officer, had speculated that the Captain had a natural flair for the theatrical.

"That's it, lads," he sang out again, grandly pointing to starboard with his cutlass. "Run them out, run them out! Let's show them what we're made of!"

"We won't have to show them," Uncle Patch snarled as he clambered up next to him. My uncle looked more the pirate type than Captain Hunter, for he was a tall, broad-shouldered man who would have looked more at home in a boxing ring than standing over a patient. Looks can deceive, for he had a delicate touch and was well-known as one of the finest surgeons afloat. He clung to the rail and stared into the distance, shouting, "What we're made of will be apparent to all, for it presently shall be spread all over the decks! Tell me now, are we really to attack that brute?"

Hunter threw back his head and laughed long and loud, an act that never failed to annoy my uncle. Indeed, I believe that is just why Hunter did it. I ran to the starboard railing and pushed my way between sweating and swearing pirates old enough to be my grandfather. Then I just stood there with my mouth open.

The thunder I had heard hadn't been thunder.

The sun was rising up out of the east like a burning orange, the sky deep royal blue, the sea almost black. And where the sky met the water, ships were fighting with flashes of fire, billows of smoke, and seconds later, the crash of cannon fire.

I strained with the rest of the crew to see what was happening. Three of the four vessels were sloops, or at least the one still firing and the one burning were. The only mark of the third was a sinking mast and men clinging to floating debris. And in the middle . . .

Hunter bellowed, "She's flying colors, Mr. Adams. See if you can make them out!"

"Aye, aye, sir!" Mr. Adams, who in his former days had been one of the oldest midshipmen in the Royal Navy, climbed the rigging to the maintop, whipped out his telescope, and scanned the battle. So did I, but from the deck.

The great three-masted ship unleashed another broadside into the burning sloop, sending sparks and burning wood exploding into the air. Whoever the men were on it, they were no cowards. With the ship burning and sinking from under them, they managed to get off one last broadside. I rubbed my eyes. Surely the shot hadn't actually *bounced* off those towering black sides?

With hand to mouth, Mr. Hunter called up, "Are her colors red, Mr. Adams? Does she fly the red flag? Is it the Red Queen?"

The Red Queen was Jack Steele's huge warship. Was the monster before us the flagship of that pirate king? Were we going to meet face to face with him at last? The great guns boomed again and the burning sloop began to go down.

"Use your eyes!" Uncle Patch snapped. "The Queen's the color of fresh blood, but that thing's the color of old pitch!" The strange ship fired again, a shattering broadside that sent up a storm of smoke. "Devil's heart, how many guns does the beast bear?"

Then the dawning light hit the great ship's flag. It was indeed red. And gold.

"She's a Spaniard, captain!" sang out Mr. Adams. "With a spanish flag as big as Castille and gaudy as a Mexican sunset!"

Hunter had seen as well, and his shoulders sagged. I knew he had been hoping for the Red Queen and for Jack Steele, for he bore the man an ancient grudge. But with none of his disappointment showing in his voice, he called up, "And her adversaries, Mr. Adams?"

In the maintop, Mr. Adams clapped his telescope to. "Can't tell anything of the sinking ones, sir, but the one that's left flies the Jolly Roger."

"Good," Uncle Patch said with a grim nod. "So the dons are doing our job for us. More power to them, say I. Let's be off, now, and out of danger."

I stared at the massive ship as it loosed another broadside. I had never seen a Spanish warship before. She was long, broad, and tall, and gunfire erupted from at least three different decks. And she seemed strangely steady, barely rocking as the cannons fired.

"A real Spanish beauty, that one," said Mr. Jeffers,

the one-eyed gunner next to me, as he prepared his gun. He turned his head and gave me a grim smile. "Slow as Christmas in stays, but she sails as steady as a castle on a rock. The dons build them wide and heavy, they do. Not all slim and frenchified like this here skiff." Like most gunners, Mr. Jeffers felt that the whole aim of shipbuilding was to keep the guns steady.

"We have the wind gage. Bring her about, Mr. Warburton," Captain Hunter shouted to our hulking helmsman. "Stand ready for battle, men!"

"Ready for . . . ! Have you lost your senses, man?" sputtered Uncle Patch, waving his arms. "She's a hundred forty feet stem to stern if an inch, she's probably got twice as many guns as we have, and she's so broad you could berth the Aurora on her decks and not touch the rails! And she's sinking pirates! Pirates, for all love, and doing our very job for us! Leave the brute alone, William!"

Hunter grinned at him. "What, and miss this golden opportunity?"

**PIRATE HUNTER
THE GUNS OF TORTUGA**
Available March 2003

Test your detective skills with these spine-tingling Aladdin Mysteries!

The Star-Spangled Secret
By K. M. Kimball

Mystery at Kittiwake Bay
By Joyce Stengel

Scared Stiff
By Willo Davis Roberts

O'Dwyer & Grady
Starring in Acting Innocent
By Eileen Heyes

Ghosts in the Gallery
By Barbara Brooks Wallace

The York Trilogy By Phyllis Reynolds Naylor

Shadows on the Wall

Faces in the Water

Footprints at the Window

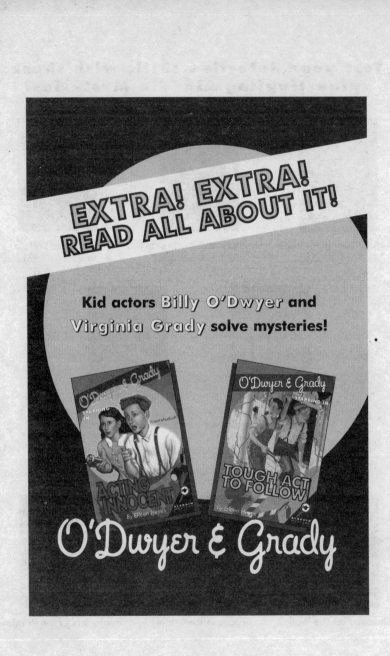